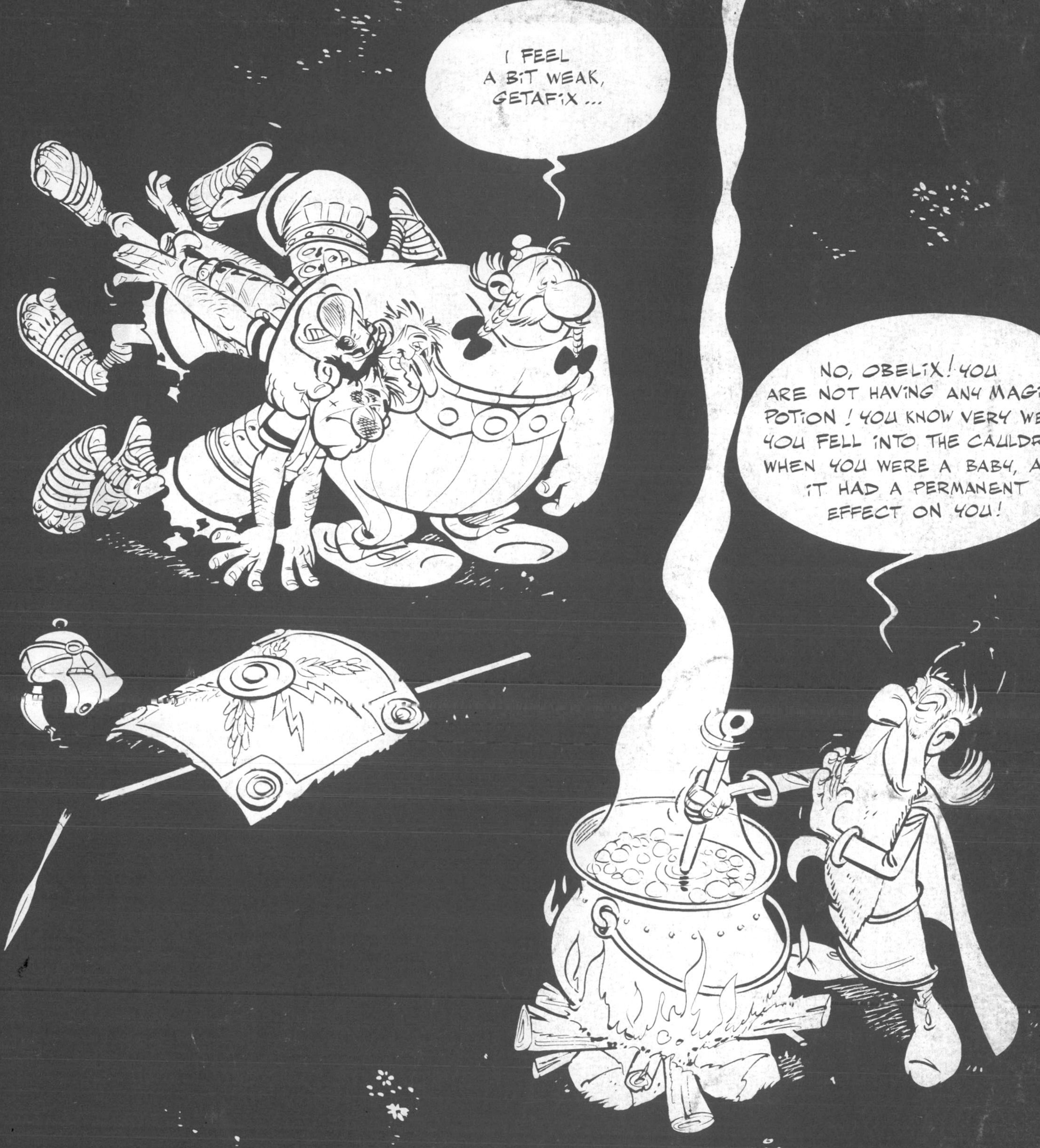
I FEEL A BIT WEAK, GETAFIX ...
NO, OBELIX! YOU ARE NOT HAVING ANY MAGIC POTION! YOU KNOW VERY WELL YOU FELL INTO THE CAULDRON WHEN YOU WERE A BABY, AND IT HAD A PERMANENT EFFECT ON YOU!

GOSCINNY AND UDERZO

PRESENT

An Asterix Adventure

ASTERIX AND THE ACTRESS

à Hugo
mon Petit-fils

Original title: *Astérix et Latraviata*

Original edition © 2001 Les Éditions Albert René / Goscinny-Uderzo
English translation © 2001 Les Éditions Albert René / Goscinny-Uderzo

Exclusive licensee: Orion Publishing Group
Translators: Anthea Bell and Derek Hockridge
Typography: Bryony Newhouse
Inking: Fréderic Mébarki
Colour work: Thierry Mébarki
Co-ordination: Studio 'Et Cetera'

The right of Goscinny-Uderzo to be identified as the author of this work has been
assserted by them in accordance with the Copyright, Designs and Patents Act 1988.

Hardback edition first published in Great Britain in 2001 by Orion Books Ltd,
Orion House, 5 Upper Saint Martin's Lane, Lodnon WC2H 9EA

This edition first published in Great Britain in 2002 by Orion Books Ltd,
Orion House, 5 Upper Saint Martin's Lane, London WC2H 9EA

5 7 9 10 8 6

Printed in France by Partenaires

http://gb.asterix.com
www.orionbooks.co.uk

A CIP record for this book is available from the British Library

ISBN-13 978 0 7528 4657 4 (cased)
ISBN-10 0 7528 4657 4 (cased)
ISBN-13 978 0 7528 4658 2 (paperback)
ISBN-10 0 7528 4658 2 (paperback)

Distributed in the United States of America by Sterling Publishing Co. Inc.
387 Park Avenue South, New York, NY 10016

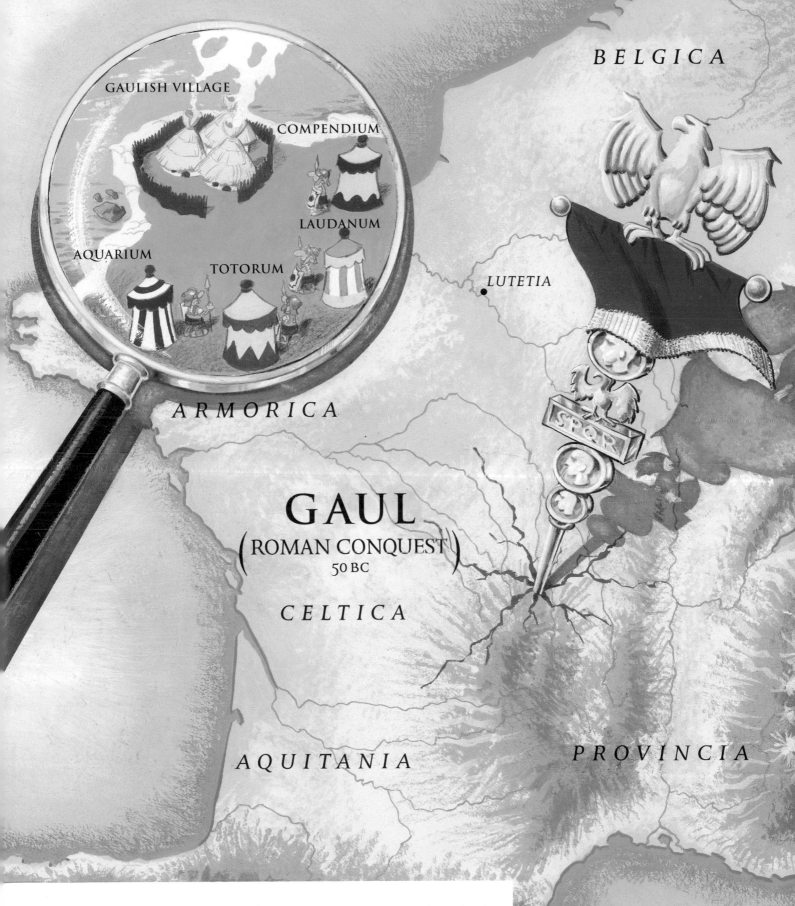

GAUL

(ROMAN CONQUEST)

50 BC

BELGICA

ARMORICA

CELTICA

AQUITANIA

PROVINCIA

LUTETIA

GAULISH VILLAGE

COMPENDIUM

LAUDANUM

AQUARIUM

TOTORUM

THE YEAR IS 50 BC. GAUL IS ENTIRELY OCCUPIED BY THE ROMANS. WELL, NOT ENTIRELY...ONE SMALL VILLAGE OF THE INDOMITABLE GAULS STILL HOLDS OUT AGAINST THE INVADERS. AND LIFE IS NOT EASY FOR THE ROMAN LEGIONARIES WHO GARRISON THE FORTIFIED CAMPS OF TOTORUM, AQUARIUM, LAUDANUM AND COMPENDIUM...

ASTERIX, THE HERO OF THESE ADVENTURES. A SHREWD, CUNNING LITTLE WARRIOR, ALL PERILOUS MISSIONS ARE IMMEDIATELY ENTRUSTED TO HIM. ASTERIX GETS HIS SUPERHUMAN STRENGTH FROM THE MAGIC POTION BREWED BY THE DRUID GETAFIX . . .

OBELIX, ASTERIX'S INSEPARABLE FRIEND. A MENHIR DELIVERY-MAN BY TRADE, ADDICTED TO WILD BOAR. OBELIX IS ALWAYS READY TO DROP EVERYTHING AND GO OFF ON A NEW ADVENTURE WITH ASTERIX – SO LONG AS THERE'S WILD BOAR TO EAT, AND PLENTY OF FIGHTING. HIS CONSTANT COMPANION IS DOGMATIX, THE ONLY KNOWN CANINE ECOLOGIST, WHO HOWLS WITH DESPAIR WHEN A TREE IS CUT DOWN.

GETAFIX, THE VENERABLE VILLAGE DRUID, GATHERS MISTLETOE AND BREWS MAGIC POTIONS. HIS SPECIALITY IS THE POTION WHICH GIVES THE DRINKER SUPERHUMAN STRENGTH. BUT GETAFIX ALSO HAS OTHER RECIPES UP HIS SLEEVE . . .

CACOFONIX, THE BARD. OPINION IS DIVIDED AS TO HIS MUSICAL GIFTS. CACOFONIX THINKS HE'S A GENIUS. EVERY-ONE ELSE THINKS HE'S UNSPEAKABLE. BUT SO LONG AS HE DOESN'T SPEAK, LET ALONE SING, EVERYBODY LIKES HIM . . .

FINALLY, VITALSTATISTIX, THE CHIEF OF THE TRIBE. MAJESTIC, BRAVE AND HOT-TEMPERED, THE OLD WARRIOR IS RESPECTED BY HIS MEN AND FEARED BY HIS ENEMIES. VITALSTATISTIX HIMSELF HAS ONLY ONE FEAR, HE IS AFRAID THE SKY MAY FALL ON HIS HEAD TOMORROW. BUT AS HE ALWAYS SAYS, TOMORROW NEVER COMES.

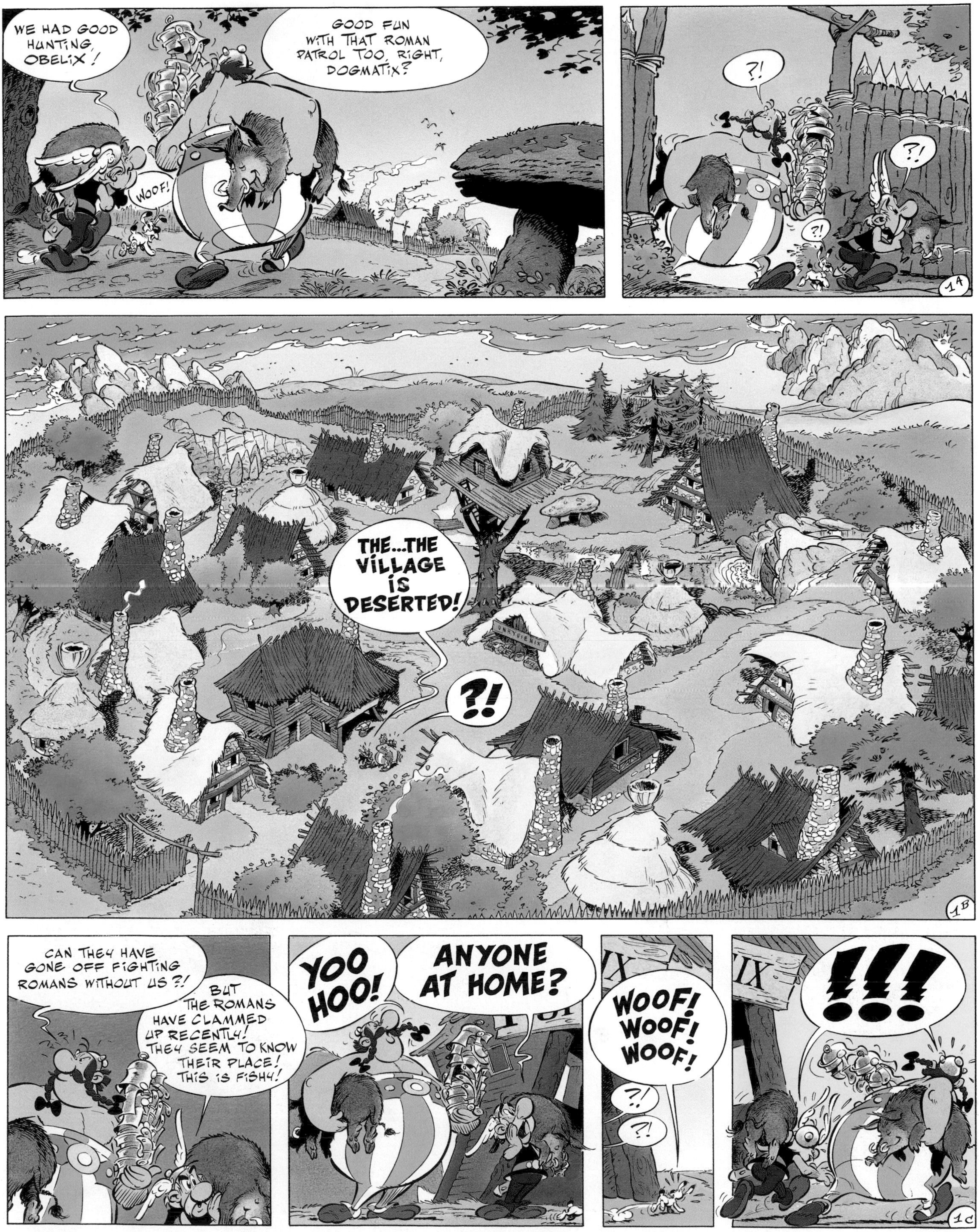

WE HAD GOOD HUNTING, OBELIX!
GOOD FUN WITH THAT ROMAN PATROL TOO, RIGHT, DOGMATIX?
WOOF!
?!
?!
?!
THE...THE VILLAGE IS DESERTED!
?!
CAN THEY HAVE GONE OFF FIGHTING ROMANS WITHOUT US ?!
BUT THE ROMANS HAVE CLAMMED UP RECENTLY! THEY SEEM TO KNOW THEIR PLACE! THIS IS FISHY!
YOO HOO!
ANYONE AT HOME?
WOOF! WOOF! WOOF!
?!
?!
!!!

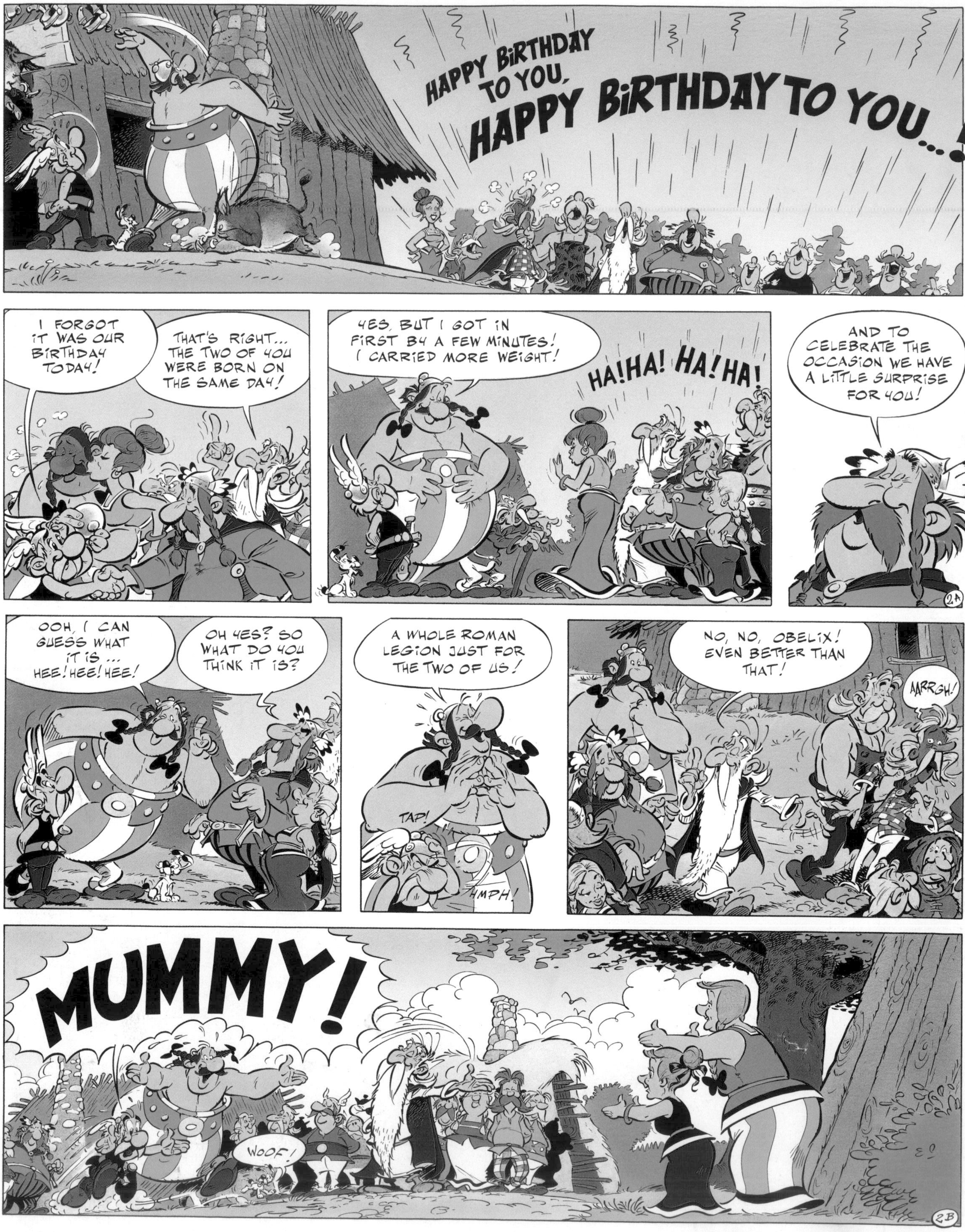
HAPPY BIRTHDAY TO YOU, HAPPY BIRTHDAY TO YOU...!
I FORGOT IT WAS OUR BIRTHDAY TODAY!
THAT'S RIGHT... THE TWO OF YOU WERE BORN ON THE SAME DAY!
YES, BUT I GOT IN FIRST BY A FEW MINUTES! I CARRIED MORE WEIGHT!
HA!HA! HA!HA!
AND TO CELEBRATE THE OCCASION WE HAVE A LITTLE SURPRISE FOR YOU!
OOH, I CAN GUESS WHAT IT IS ... HEE! HEE! HEE!
OH YES? SO WHAT DO YOU THINK IT IS?
A WHOLE ROMAN LEGION JUST FOR THE TWO OF US!
TAP!
HMPH!
NO, NO, OBELIX! EVEN BETTER THAN THAT!
AARRGH!
MUMMY!
WOOF!

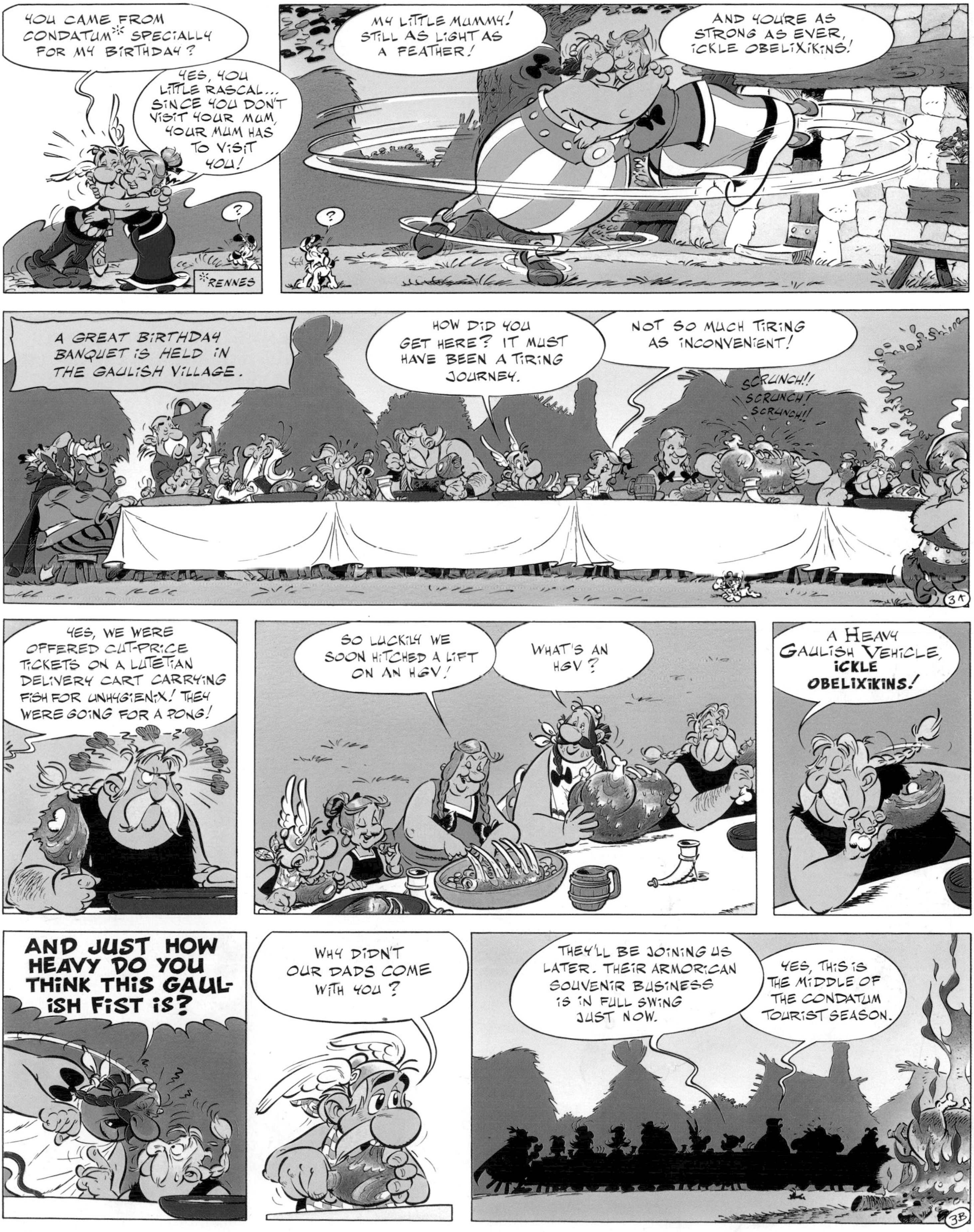

YOU CAME FROM CONDATUM* SPECIALLY FOR MY BIRTHDAY?
YES, YOU LITTLE RASCAL... SINCE YOU DON'T VISIT YOUR MUM, YOUR MUM HAS TO VISIT YOU!
?
*RENNES
MY LITTLE MUMMY! STILL AS LIGHT AS A FEATHER!
AND YOU'RE AS STRONG AS EVER, ICKLE OBELIXIKINS!
?
A GREAT BIRTHDAY BANQUET IS HELD IN THE GAULISH VILLAGE.
HOW DID YOU GET HERE? IT MUST HAVE BEEN A TIRING JOURNEY.
NOT SO MUCH TIRING AS INCONVENIENT!
SCRUNCH!! SCRUNCH! SCRUNCH!!
3A
YES, WE WERE OFFERED CUT-PRICE TICKETS ON A LUTETIAN DELIVERY CART CARRYING FISH FOR UNHYGIENIX! THEY WERE GOING FOR A PONG!
SO LUCKILY WE SOON HITCHED A LIFT ON AN HGV!
WHAT'S AN HGV?
A HEAVY GAULISH VEHICLE, ICKLE OBELIXIKINS!
AND JUST HOW HEAVY DO YOU THINK THIS GAULISH FIST IS?
WHY DIDN'T OUR DADS COME WITH YOU?
THEY'LL BE JOINING US LATER. THEIR ARMORICAN SOUVENIR BUSINESS IS IN FULL SWING JUST NOW.
YES, THIS IS THE MIDDLE OF THE CONDATUM TOURIST SEASON.
3B

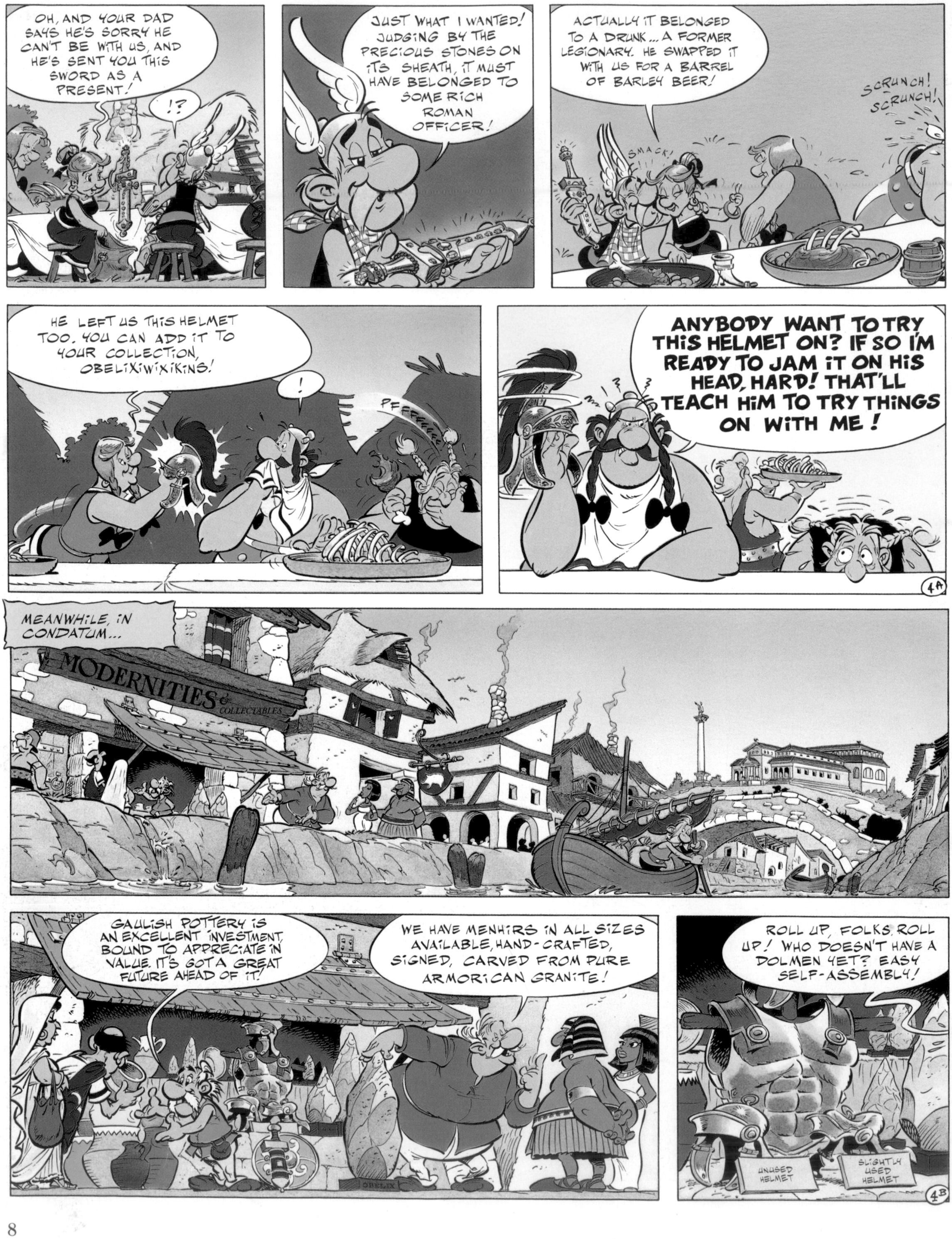
OH, AND YOUR DAD SAYS HE'S SORRY HE CAN'T BE WITH US, AND HE'S SENT YOU THIS SWORD AS A PRESENT!
!?
JUST WHAT I WANTED! JUDGING BY THE PRECIOUS STONES ON ITS SHEATH, IT MUST HAVE BELONGED TO SOME RICH ROMAN OFFICER!
ACTUALLY IT BELONGED TO A DRUNK... A FORMER LEGIONARY. HE SWAPPED IT WITH US FOR A BARREL OF BARLEY BEER!
SMACK!
SCRUNCH! SCRUNCH!
HE LEFT US THIS HELMET TOO. YOU CAN ADD IT TO YOUR COLLECTION, OBELIXIWIXIKINS!
!
ANYBODY WANT TO TRY THIS HELMET ON? IF SO I'M READY TO JAM IT ON HIS HEAD, HARD! THAT'LL TEACH HIM TO TRY THINGS ON WITH ME!
4A
MEANWHILE, IN CONDATUM...
MODERNITIES & COLLECTABLES
GAULISH POTTERY IS AN EXCELLENT INVESTMENT, BOUND TO APPRECIATE IN VALUE. IT'S GOT A GREAT FUTURE AHEAD OF IT!
WE HAVE MENHIRS IN ALL SIZES AVAILABLE, HAND-CRAFTED, SIGNED, CARVED FROM PURE ARMORICAN GRANITE!
OBELIX
ROLL UP, FOLKS. ROLL UP! WHO DOESN'T HAVE A DOLMEN YET? EASY SELF-ASSEMBLY!
UNUSED HELMET
SLIGHTLY USED HELMET
4B

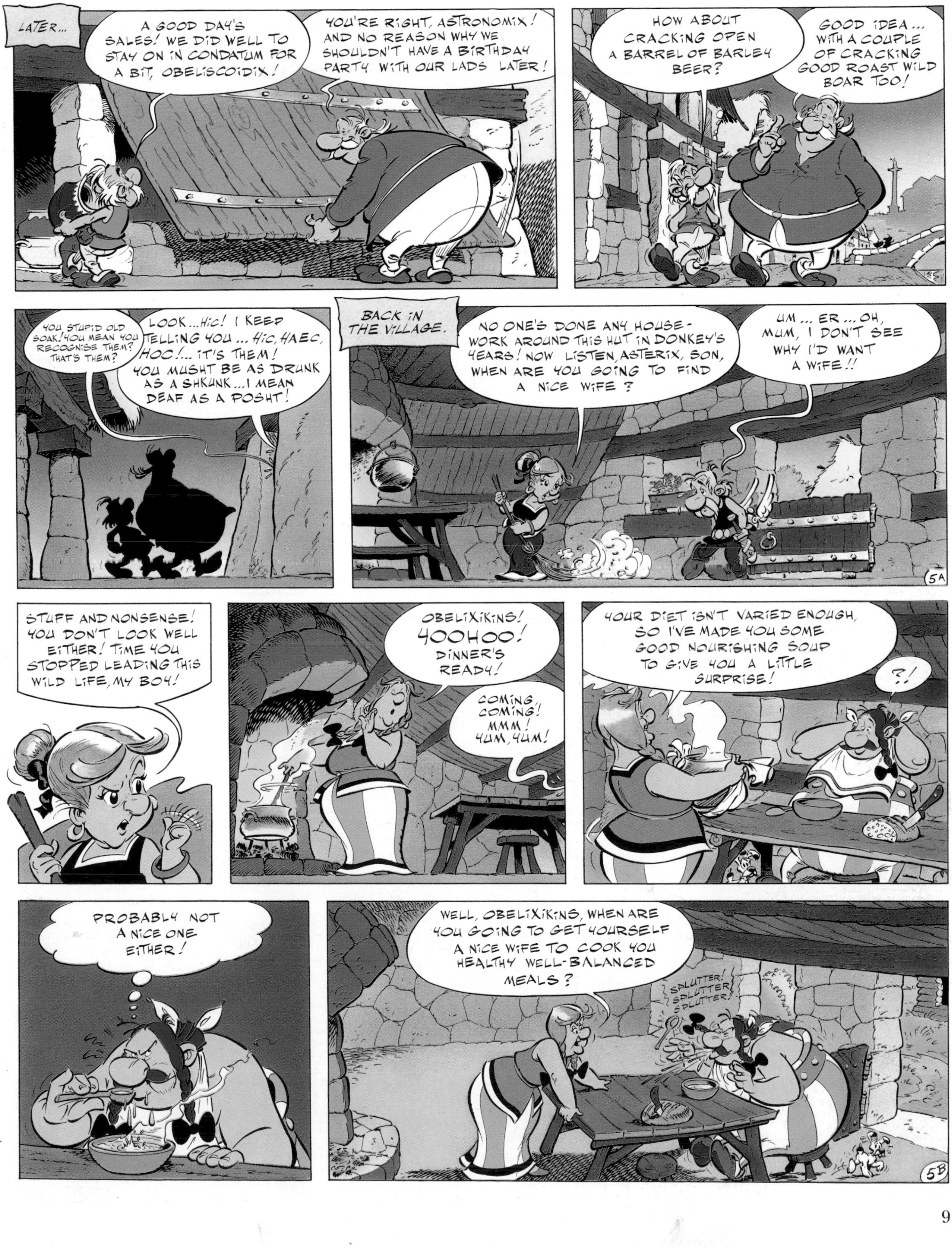
LATER...
A GOOD DAY'S SALES! WE DID WELL TO STAY ON IN CONDATUM FOR A BIT, OBELISCOIDIX!
YOU'RE RIGHT, ASTRONOMIX! AND NO REASON WHY WE SHOULDN'T HAVE A BIRTHDAY PARTY WITH OUR LADS LATER!
HOW ABOUT CRACKING OPEN A BARREL OF BARLEY BEER?
GOOD IDEA... WITH A COUPLE OF CRACKING GOOD ROAST WILD BOAR TOO!
YOU STUPID OLD SOAK! YOU MEAN YOU RECOGNISE THEM? THAT'S THEM?
LOOK...HIC! I KEEP TELLING YOU... HIC, HAEC, HOC!... IT'S THEM! YOU MUSHT BE AS DRUNK AS A SHKUNK... I MEAN DEAF AS A POSHT!
BACK IN THE VILLAGE.
NO ONE'S DONE ANY HOUSE-WORK AROUND THIS HUT IN DONKEY'S YEARS! NOW LISTEN, ASTERIX, SON, WHEN ARE YOU GOING TO FIND A NICE WIFE?
UM... ER... OH, MUM, I DON'T SEE WHY I'D WANT A WIFE!!
5A
STUFF AND NONSENSE! YOU DON'T LOOK WELL EITHER! TIME YOU STOPPED LEADING THIS WILD LIFE, MY BOY!
OBELIXIKINS! YOOHOO! DINNER'S READY!
COMING, COMING! MMM! YUM, YUM!
YOUR DIET ISN'T VARIED ENOUGH, SO I'VE MADE YOU SOME GOOD NOURISHING SOUP TO GIVE YOU A LITTLE SURPRISE!
?!
PROBABLY NOT A NICE ONE EITHER!
WELL, OBELIXIKINS, WHEN ARE YOU GOING TO GET YOURSELF A NICE WIFE TO COOK YOU HEALTHY WELL-BALANCED MEALS?
SPLUTTER! SPLUTTER! SPLUTTER!
5B

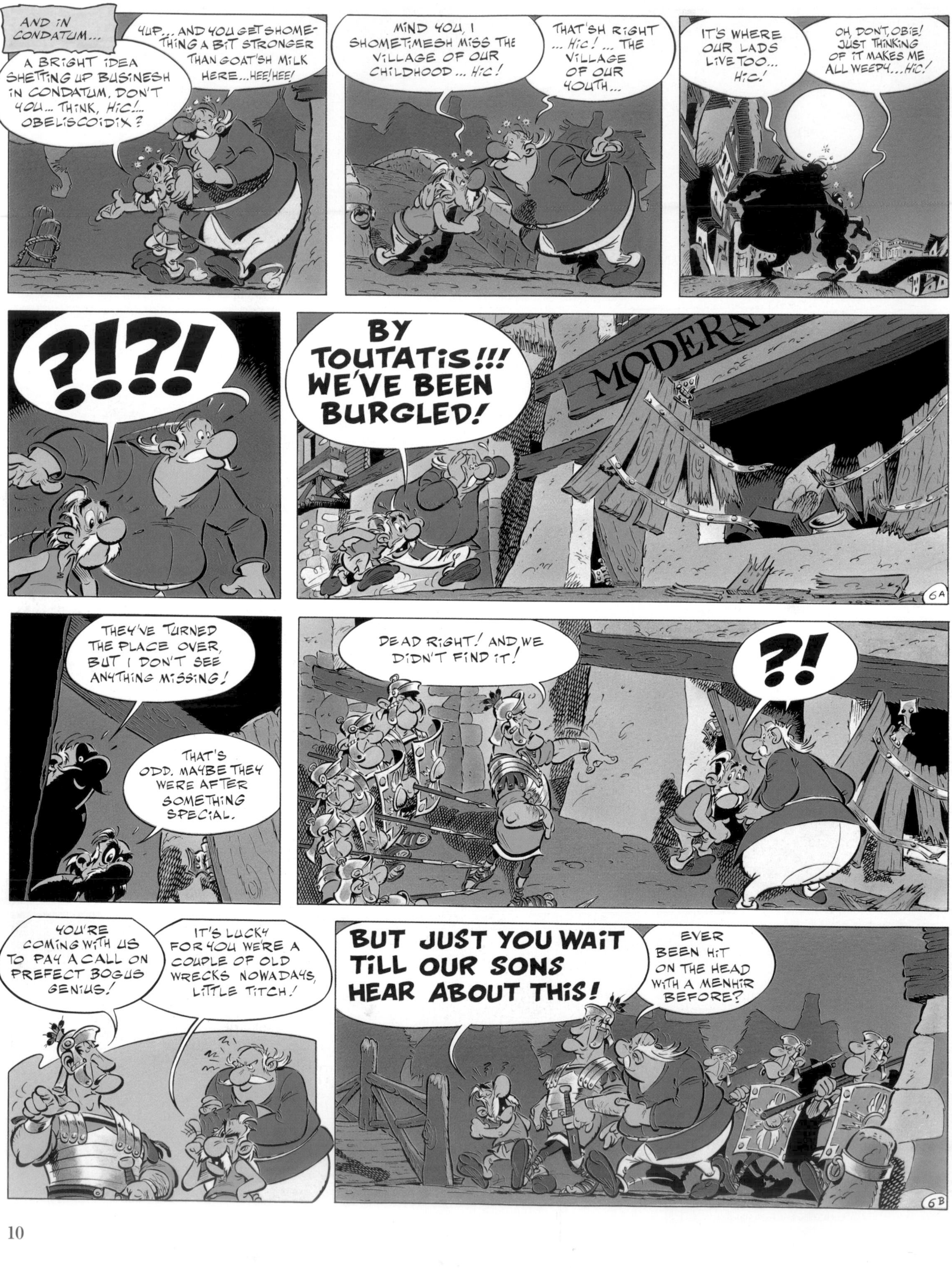

AND IN CONDATUM...
A BRIGHT IDEA SHETTING UP BUSINESH IN CONDATUM, DON'T YOU... THINK, HIC!... OBELISCOIDIX?
YUP... AND YOU GET SHOMETHING A BIT STRONGER THAN GOAT'SH MILK HERE... HEE! HEE!
MIND YOU, I SHOMETIMESH MISS THE VILLAGE OF OUR CHILDHOOD... HIC!
THAT'SH RIGHT ... HIC! ... THE VILLAGE OF OUR YOUTH...
IT'S WHERE OUR LADS LIVE TOO... HIC!
OH, DON'T, OBIE! JUST THINKING OF IT MAKES ME ALL WEEPY... HIC!
?!?!
BY TOUTATIS!!! WE'VE BEEN BURGLED!
MODERN
THEY'VE TURNED THE PLACE OVER, BUT I DON'T SEE ANYTHING MISSING!
THAT'S ODD. MAYBE THEY WERE AFTER SOMETHING SPECIAL.
DEAD RIGHT! AND WE DIDN'T FIND IT!
?!
YOU'RE COMING WITH US TO PAY A CALL ON OLD PREFECT BOGUS GENIUS!
IT'S LUCKY FOR YOU WE'RE A COUPLE OF OLD WRECKS NOWADAYS, LITTLE TITCH!
BUT JUST YOU WAIT TILL OUR SONS HEAR ABOUT THIS!
EVER BEEN HIT ON THE HEAD WITH A MENHIR BEFORE?

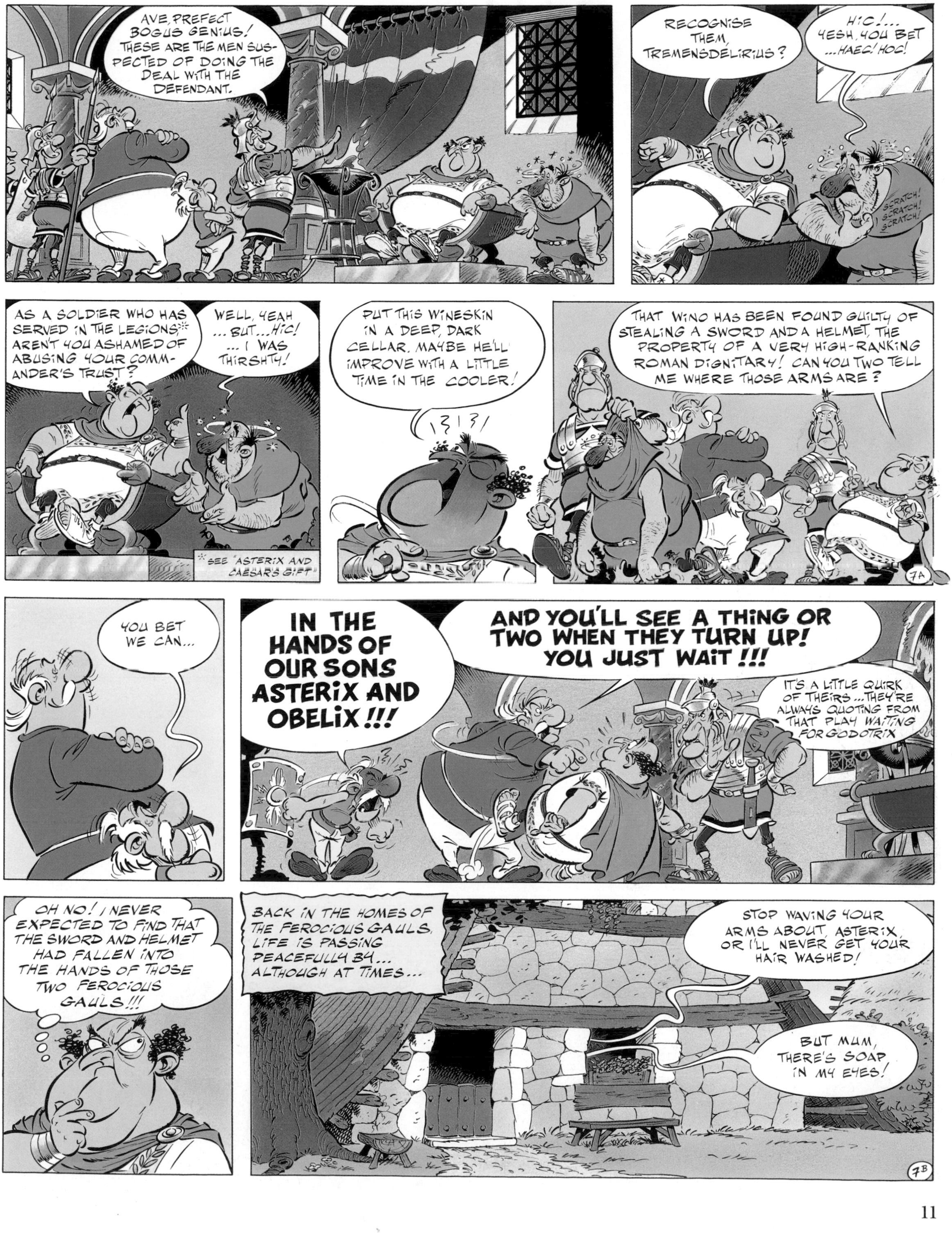
AVE, PREFECT BOGUS GENIUS! THESE ARE THE MEN SUSPECTED OF DOING THE DEAL WITH THE DEFENDANT.
RECOGNISE THEM, TREMENSDELIRIUS?
HIC!... YESH, YOU BET ...HAEC! HOC!
SCRATCH! SCRATCH! SCRATCH!
AS A SOLDIER WHO HAS SERVED IN THE LEGIONS,* AREN'T YOU ASHAMED OF ABUSING YOUR COMMANDER'S TRUST?
WELL, YEAH ... BUT... HIC! ... I WAS THIRSHTY!
* SEE "ASTERIX AND CAESAR'S GIFT"
PUT THIS WINESKIN IN A DEEP, DARK CELLAR. MAYBE HE'LL IMPROVE WITH A LITTLE TIME IN THE COOLER!
THAT WINO HAS BEEN FOUND GUILTY OF STEALING A SWORD AND A HELMET, THE PROPERTY OF A VERY HIGH-RANKING ROMAN DIGNITARY! CAN YOU TWO TELL ME WHERE THOSE ARMS ARE?
7A
YOU BET WE CAN...
IN THE HANDS OF OUR SONS ASTERIX AND OBELIX!!!
AND YOU'LL SEE A THING OR TWO WHEN THEY TURN UP! YOU JUST WAIT!!!
IT'S A LITTLE QUIRK OF THEIRS... THEY'RE ALWAYS QUOTING FROM THAT PLAY WAITING FOR GODOTRIX
OH NO! I NEVER EXPECTED TO FIND THAT THE SWORD AND HELMET HAD FALLEN INTO THE HANDS OF THOSE TWO FEROCIOUS GAULS!!!
BACK IN THE HOMES OF THE FEROCIOUS GAULS, LIFE IS PASSING PEACEFULLY BY... ALTHOUGH AT TIMES...
STOP WAVING YOUR ARMS ABOUT, ASTERIX, OR I'LL NEVER GET YOUR HAIR WASHED!
BUT MUM, THERE'S SOAP IN MY EYES!
7B

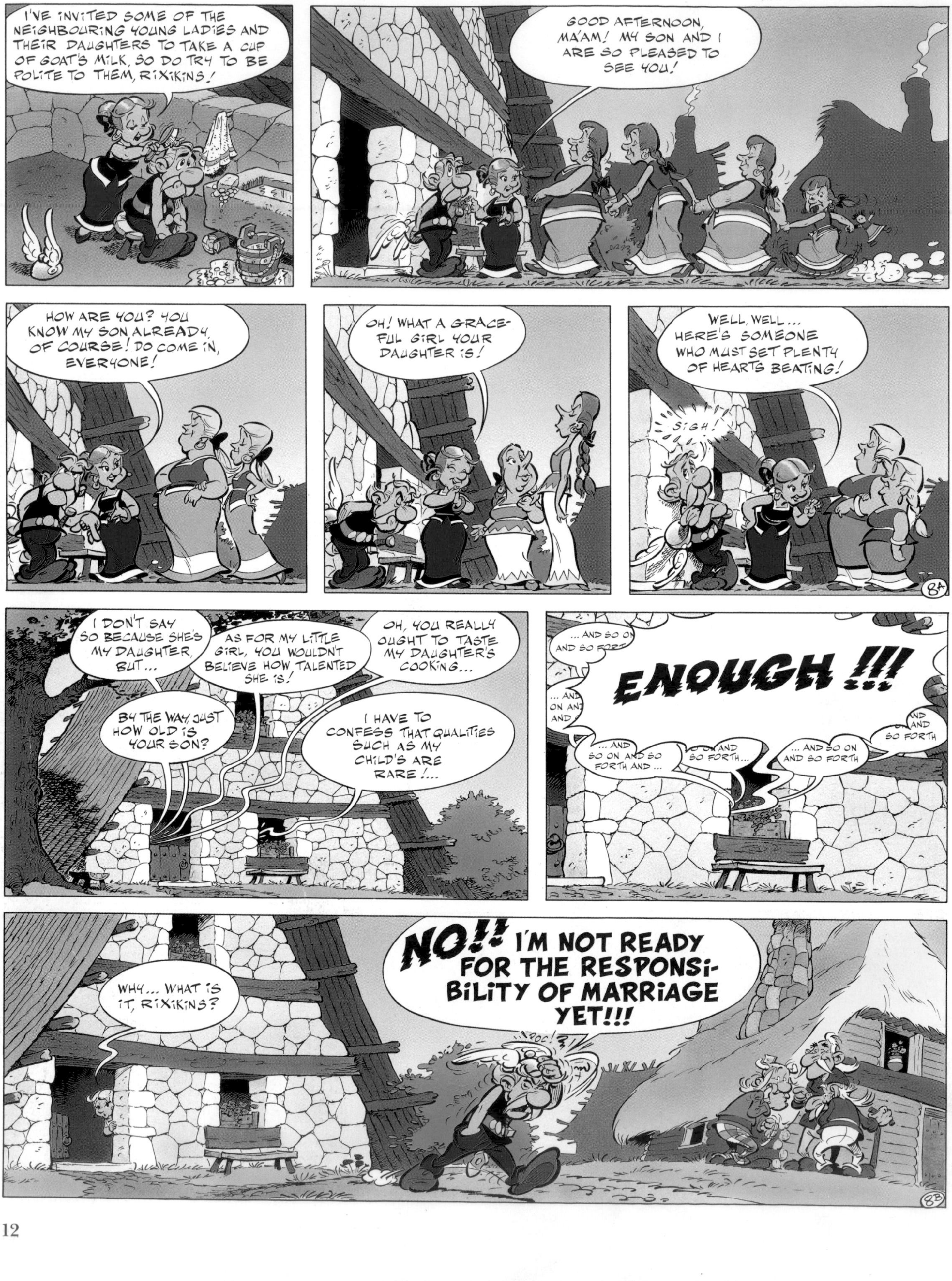
I'VE INVITED SOME OF THE NEIGHBOURING YOUNG LADIES AND THEIR DAUGHTERS TO TAKE A CUP OF GOAT'S MILK, SO DO TRY TO BE POLITE TO THEM, RIXIKINS!
GOOD AFTERNOON, MA'AM! MY SON AND I ARE SO PLEASED TO SEE YOU!
HOW ARE YOU? YOU KNOW MY SON ALREADY, OF COURSE! DO COME IN, EVERYONE!
OH! WHAT A GRACEFUL GIRL YOUR DAUGHTER IS!
WELL, WELL... HERE'S SOMEONE WHO MUST SET PLENTY OF HEARTS BEATING!
SIGH!
8A
I DON'T SAY SO BECAUSE SHE'S MY DAUGHTER, BUT...
AS FOR MY LITTLE GIRL, YOU WOULDN'T BELIEVE HOW TALENTED SHE IS!
OH, YOU REALLY OUGHT TO TASTE MY DAUGHTER'S COOKING...
BY THE WAY, JUST HOW OLD IS YOUR SON?
I HAVE TO CONFESS THAT QUALITIES SUCH AS MY CHILD'S ARE RARE!...
... AND SO ON AND SO FORTH
ENOUGH!!!
... AND SO ON AND SO FORTH AND ...
SO FORTH...
... AND SO ON AND SO FORTH
AND SO FORTH
WHY... WHAT IS IT, RIXIKINS?
NO!! I'M NOT READY FOR THE RESPONSIBILITY OF MARRIAGE YET!!!
POC!
8B

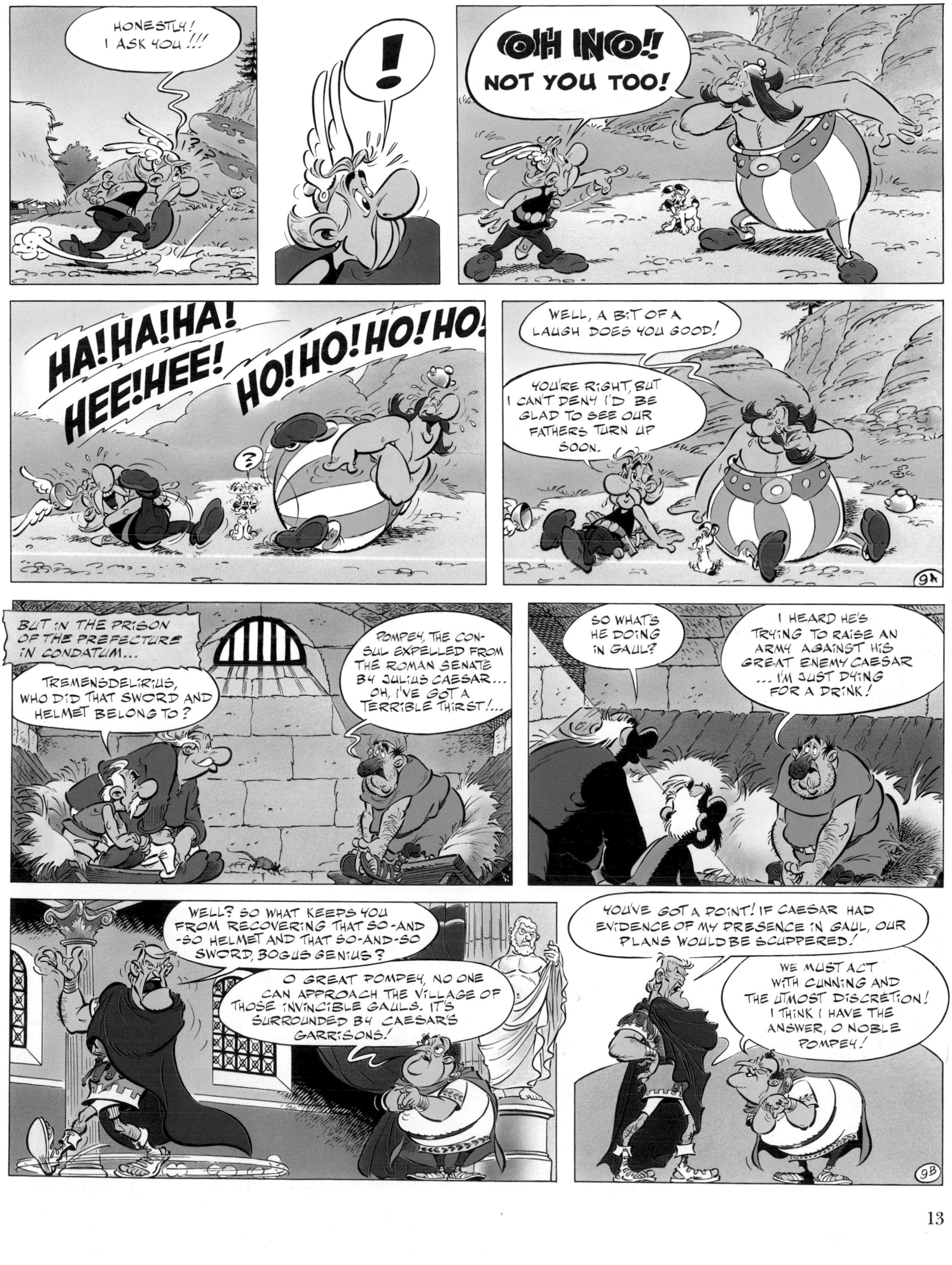
HONESTLY! I ASK YOU!!!
!
OH NO!! NOT YOU TOO!
HA!HA!HA! HEE!HEE! HO!HO!HO!HO!
?
WELL, A BIT OF A LAUGH DOES YOU GOOD!
YOU'RE RIGHT, BUT I CAN'T DENY I'D BE GLAD TO SEE OUR FATHERS TURN UP SOON.
9A
BUT IN THE PRISON OF THE PREFECTURE IN CONDATUM...
TREMENSDELIRIUS, WHO DID THAT SWORD AND HELMET BELONG TO?
POMPEY. THE CONSUL EXPELLED FROM THE ROMAN SENATE BY JULIUS CAESAR... OH, I'VE GOT A TERRIBLE THIRST!...
SO WHAT'S HE DOING IN GAUL?
I HEARD HE'S TRYING TO RAISE AN ARMY AGAINST HIS GREAT ENEMY CAESAR ... I'M JUST DYING FOR A DRINK!
WELL? SO WHAT KEEPS YOU FROM RECOVERING THAT SO-AND-SO HELMET AND THAT SO-AND-SO SWORD, BOGUS GENIUS?
O GREAT POMPEY, NO ONE CAN APPROACH THE VILLAGE OF THOSE INVINCIBLE GAULS. IT'S SURROUNDED BY CAESAR'S GARRISONS!
YOU'VE GOT A POINT! IF CAESAR HAD EVIDENCE OF MY PRESENCE IN GAUL, OUR PLANS WOULD BE SCUPPERED!
WE MUST ACT WITH CUNNING AND THE UTMOST DISCRETION! I THINK I HAVE THE ANSWER, O NOBLE POMPEY!
9B

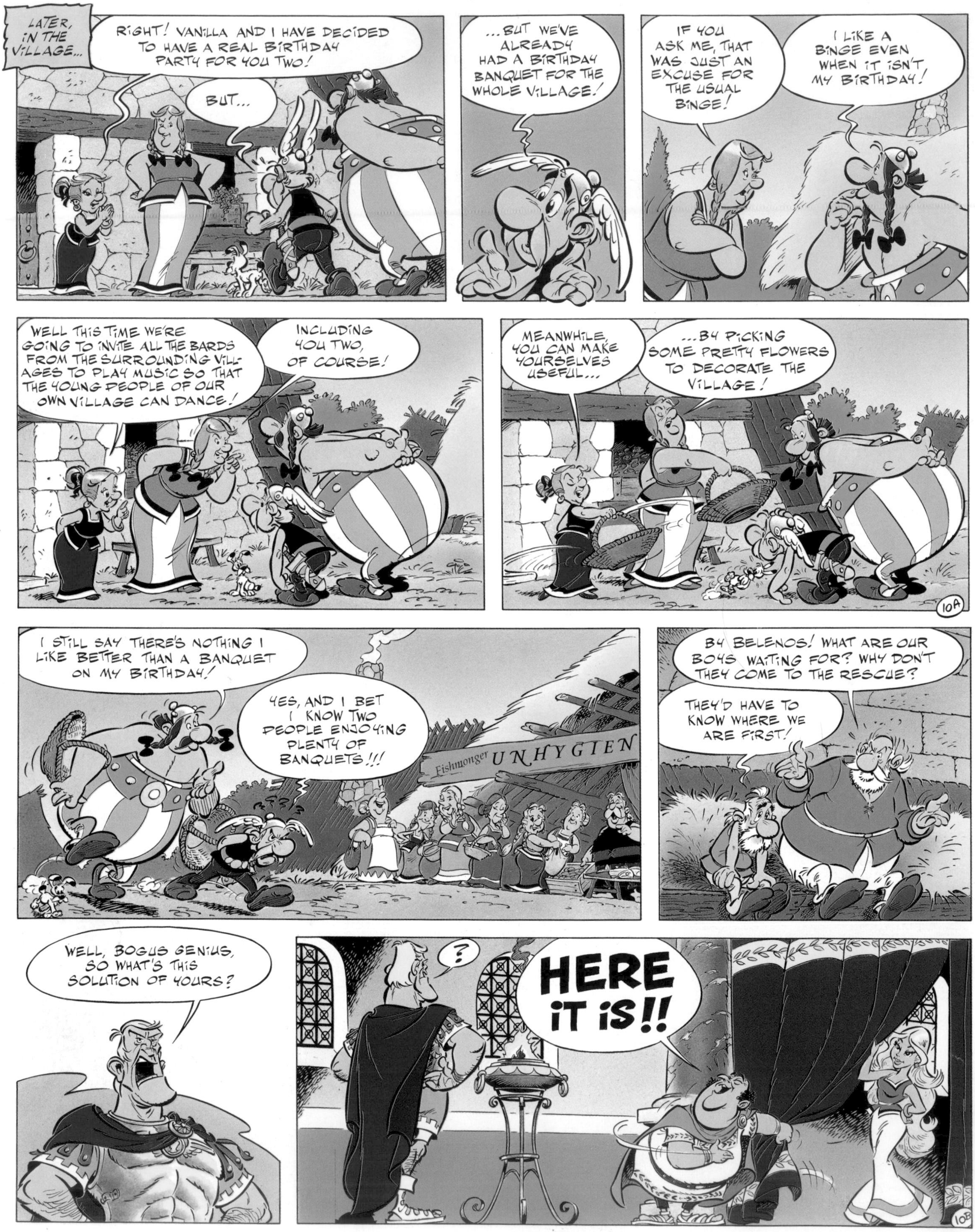
LATER, IN THE VILLAGE...
RIGHT! VANILLA AND I HAVE DECIDED TO HAVE A REAL BIRTHDAY PARTY FOR YOU TWO!
BUT...
...BUT WE'VE ALREADY HAD A BIRTHDAY BANQUET FOR THE WHOLE VILLAGE!
IF YOU ASK ME, THAT WAS JUST AN EXCUSE FOR THE USUAL BINGE!
I LIKE A BINGE EVEN WHEN IT ISN'T MY BIRTHDAY!
WELL THIS TIME WE'RE GOING TO INVITE ALL THE BARDS FROM THE SURROUNDING VILLAGES TO PLAY MUSIC SO THAT THE YOUNG PEOPLE OF OUR OWN VILLAGE CAN DANCE!
INCLUDING YOU TWO, OF COURSE!
MEANWHILE, YOU CAN MAKE YOURSELVES USEFUL...
...BY PICKING SOME PRETTY FLOWERS TO DECORATE THE VILLAGE!
10A
I STILL SAY THERE'S NOTHING I LIKE BETTER THAN A BANQUET ON MY BIRTHDAY!
YES, AND I BET I KNOW TWO PEOPLE ENJOYING PLENTY OF BANQUETS!!!
Fishmonger UNHYGIEN
BY BELENOS! WHAT ARE OUR BOYS WAITING FOR? WHY DON'T THEY COME TO THE RESCUE?
THEY'D HAVE TO KNOW WHERE WE ARE FIRST!
WELL, BOGUS GENIUS, SO WHAT'S THIS SOLUTION OF YOURS?
?
HERE IT IS!!
10B

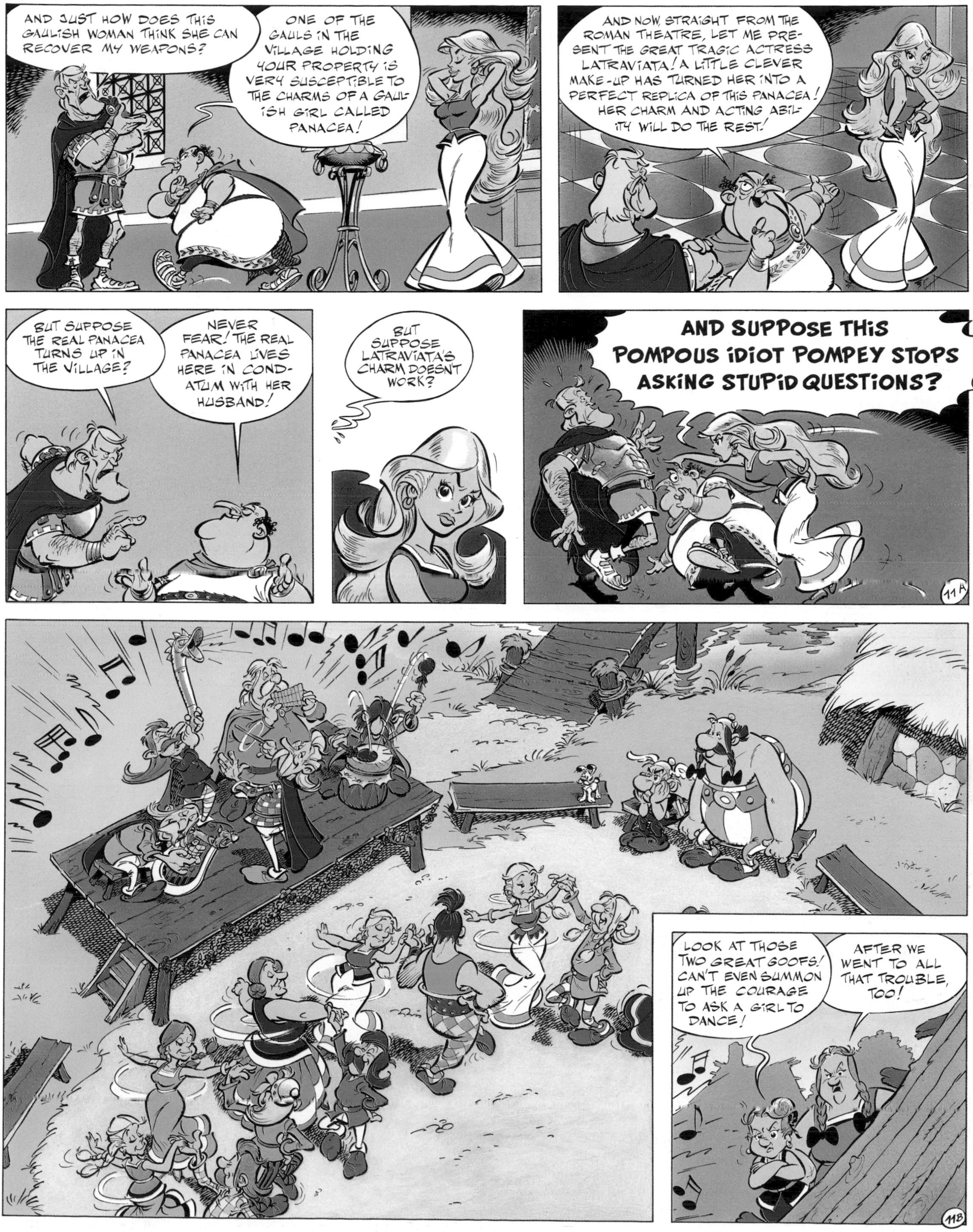
AND JUST HOW DOES THIS GAULISH WOMAN THINK SHE CAN RECOVER MY WEAPONS?
ONE OF THE GAULS IN THE VILLAGE HOLDING YOUR PROPERTY IS VERY SUSCEPTIBLE TO THE CHARMS OF A GAULISH GIRL CALLED PANACEA!
AND NOW, STRAIGHT FROM THE ROMAN THEATRE, LET ME PRESENT THE GREAT TRAGIC ACTRESS LATRAVIATA! A LITTLE CLEVER MAKE-UP HAS TURNED HER INTO A PERFECT REPLICA OF THIS PANACEA! HER CHARM AND ACTING ABILITY WILL DO THE REST!
BUT SUPPOSE THE REAL PANACEA TURNS UP IN THE VILLAGE?
NEVER FEAR! THE REAL PANACEA LIVES HERE IN CONDATUM WITH HER HUSBAND!
BUT SUPPOSE LATRAVIATA'S CHARM DOESN'T WORK?
AND SUPPOSE THIS POMPOUS IDIOT POMPEY STOPS ASKING STUPID QUESTIONS?
LOOK AT THOSE TWO GREAT GOOFS! CAN'T EVEN SUMMON UP THE COURAGE TO ASK A GIRL TO DANCE!
AFTER WE WENT TO ALL THAT TROUBLE, TOO!

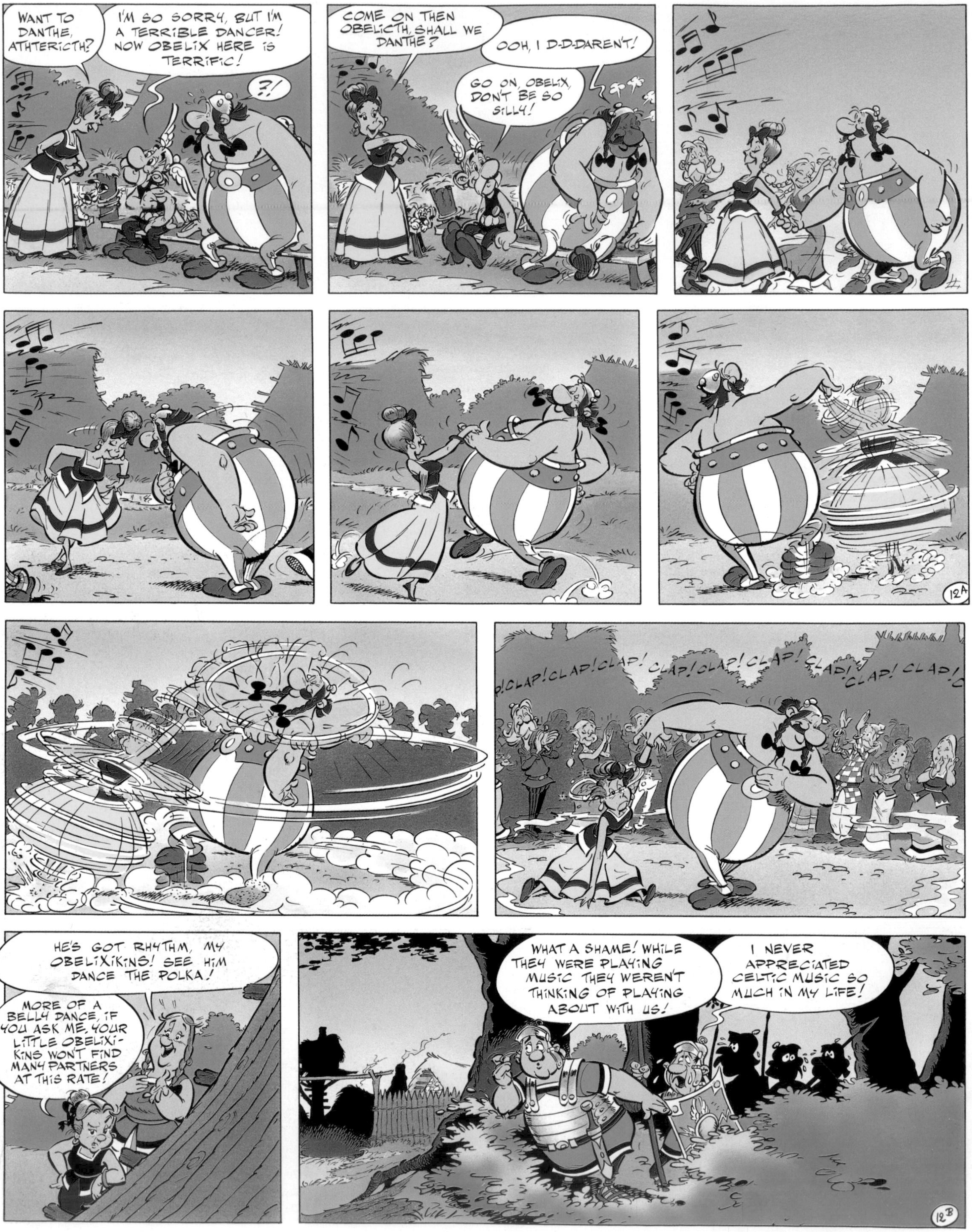
WANT TO DANTHE, ATHTERICTH?
I'M SO SORRY, BUT I'M A TERRIBLE DANCER! NOW OBELIX HERE IS TERRIFIC!
?!
COME ON THEN OBELICTH, SHALL WE DANTHE?
OOH, I D-D-DAREN'T!
GO ON, OBELIX, DON'T BE SO SILLY!
12A
CLAP! CLAP! CLAP! CLAP! CLAP! CLAP! CLAP! CLAP! CLAP!
HE'S GOT RHYTHM, MY OBELIXIKINS! SEE HIM DANCE THE POLKA!
MORE OF A BELLY DANCE, IF YOU ASK ME. YOUR LITTLE OBELIXIKINS WON'T FIND MANY PARTNERS AT THIS RATE!
WHAT A SHAME! WHILE THEY WERE PLAYING MUSIC THEY WEREN'T THINKING OF PLAYING ABOUT WITH US!
I NEVER APPRECIATED CELTIC MUSIC SO MUCH IN MY LIFE!
12B

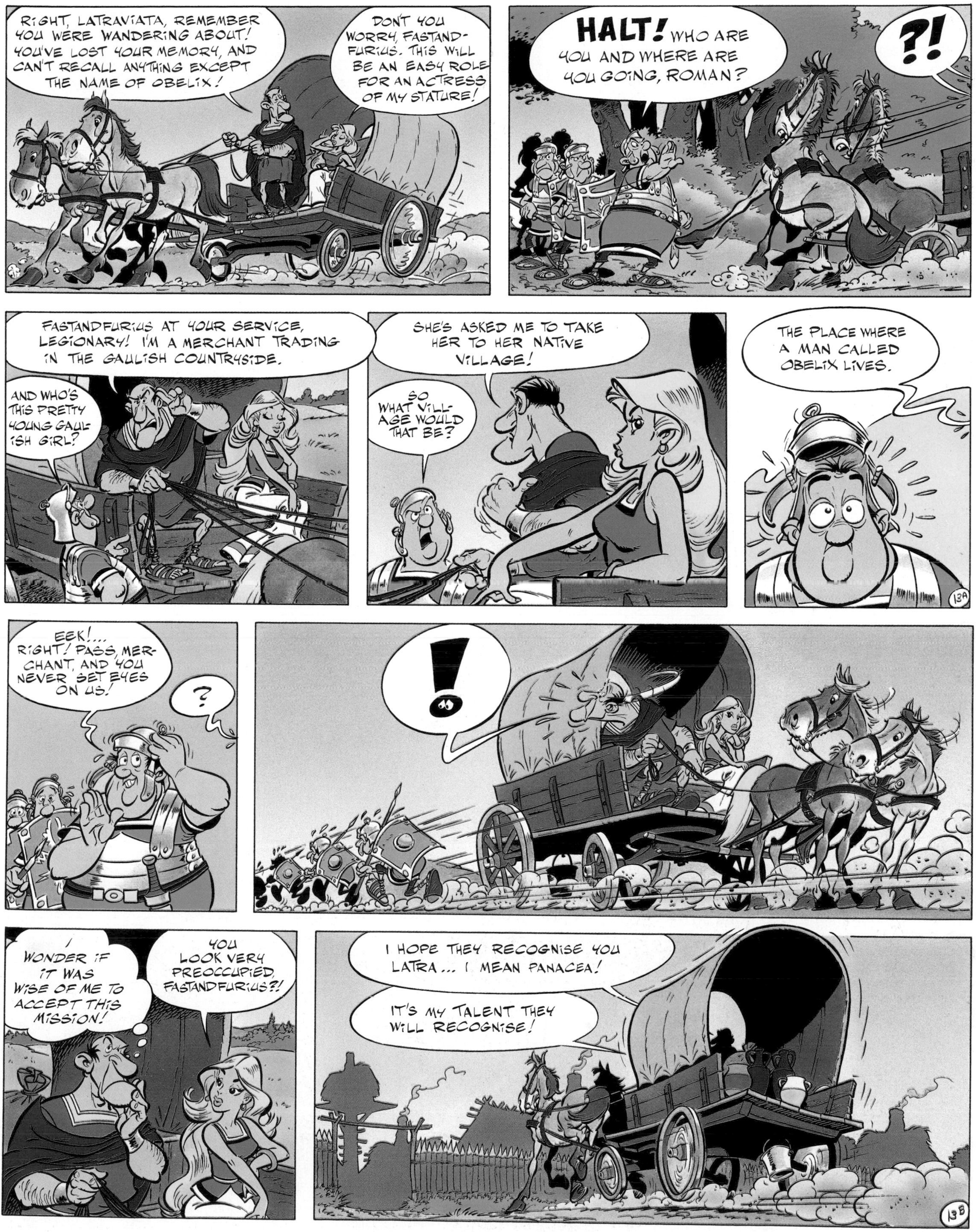
RIGHT, LATRAVIATA, REMEMBER YOU WERE WANDERING ABOUT! YOU'VE LOST YOUR MEMORY, AND CAN'T RECALL ANYTHING EXCEPT THE NAME OF OBELIX!
DON'T YOU WORRY, FASTANDFURIUS. THIS WILL BE AN EASY ROLE FOR AN ACTRESS OF MY STATURE!
HALT! WHO ARE YOU AND WHERE ARE YOU GOING, ROMAN?
?!
FASTANDFURIUS AT YOUR SERVICE, LEGIONARY! I'M A MERCHANT TRADING IN THE GAULISH COUNTRYSIDE.
AND WHO'S THIS PRETTY YOUNG GAULISH GIRL?
SHE'S ASKED ME TO TAKE HER TO HER NATIVE VILLAGE!
SO WHAT VILLAGE WOULD THAT BE?
THE PLACE WHERE A MAN CALLED OBELIX LIVES.
EEK!... RIGHT! PASS, MERCHANT, AND YOU NEVER SET EYES ON US!
?
!
I WONDER IF IT WAS WISE OF ME TO ACCEPT THIS MISSION!
YOU LOOK VERY PREOCCUPIED, FASTANDFURIUS?!
I HOPE THEY RECOGNISE YOU LATRA... I MEAN PANACEA!
IT'S MY TALENT THEY WILL RECOGNISE!

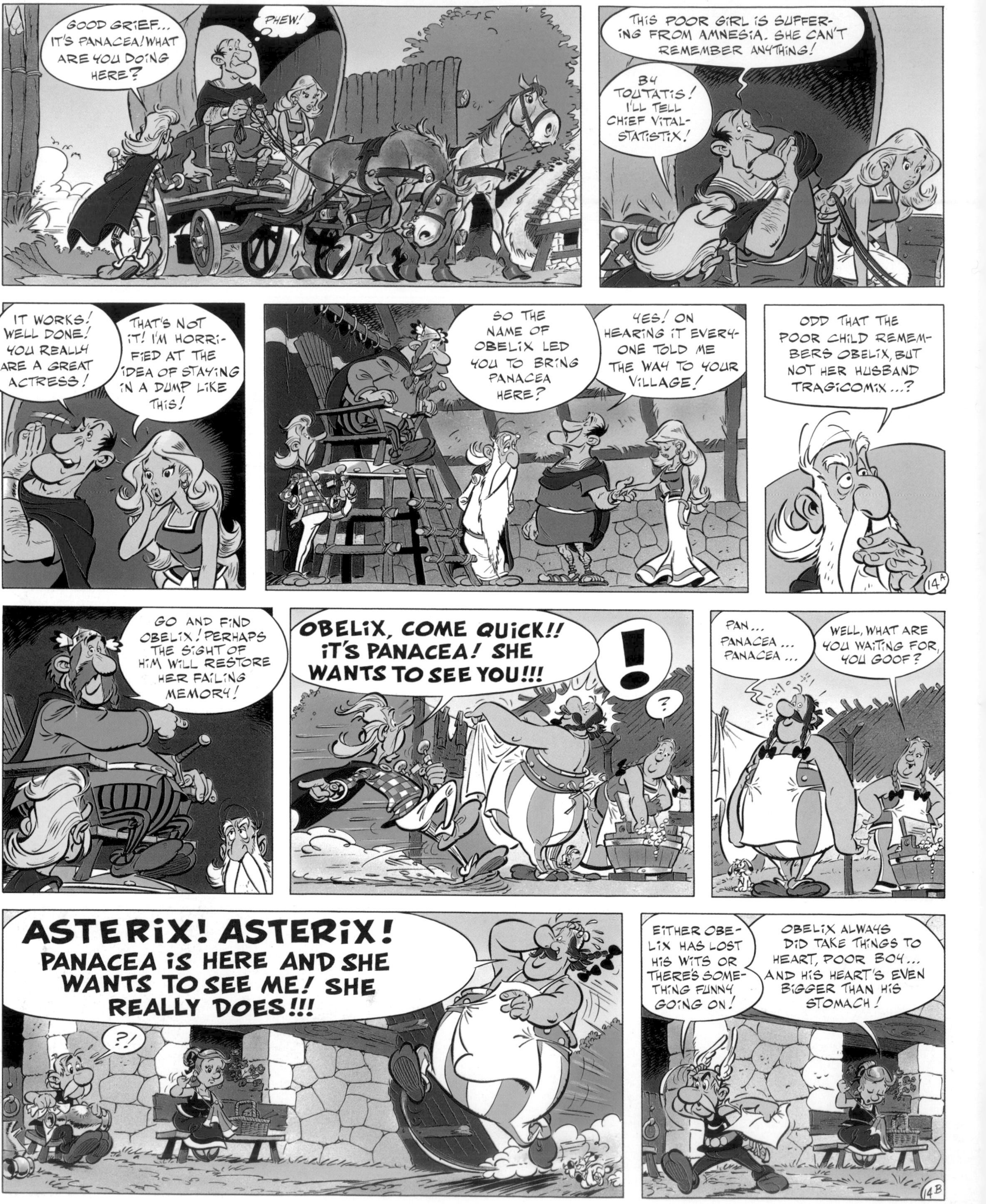
GOOD GRIEF... IT'S PANACEA! WHAT ARE YOU DOING HERE?
PHEW!
THIS POOR GIRL IS SUFFERING FROM AMNESIA. SHE CAN'T REMEMBER ANYTHING!
BY TOUTATIS! I'LL TELL CHIEF VITALSTATISTIX!
IT WORKS! WELL DONE! YOU REALLY ARE A GREAT ACTRESS!
THAT'S NOT IT! I'M HORRIFIED AT THE IDEA OF STAYING IN A DUMP LIKE THIS!
SO THE NAME OF OBELIX LED YOU TO BRING PANACEA HERE?
YES! ON HEARING IT EVERYONE TOLD ME THE WAY TO YOUR VILLAGE!
ODD THAT THE POOR CHILD REMEMBERS OBELIX, BUT NOT HER HUSBAND TRAGICOMIX...?
14A
GO AND FIND OBELIX! PERHAPS THE SIGHT OF HIM WILL RESTORE HER FAILING MEMORY!
OBELIX, COME QUICK!! IT'S PANACEA! SHE WANTS TO SEE YOU!!!
!
?
PAN... PANACEA... PANACEA...
WELL, WHAT ARE YOU WAITING FOR, YOU GOOF?
ASTERIX! ASTERIX! PANACEA IS HERE AND SHE WANTS TO SEE ME! SHE REALLY DOES!!!
?!
EITHER OBELIX HAS LOST HIS WITS OR THERE'S SOMETHING FUNNY GOING ON!
OBELIX ALWAYS DID TAKE THINGS TO HEART, POOR BOY... AND HIS HEART'S EVEN BIGGER THAN HIS STOMACH!
14B

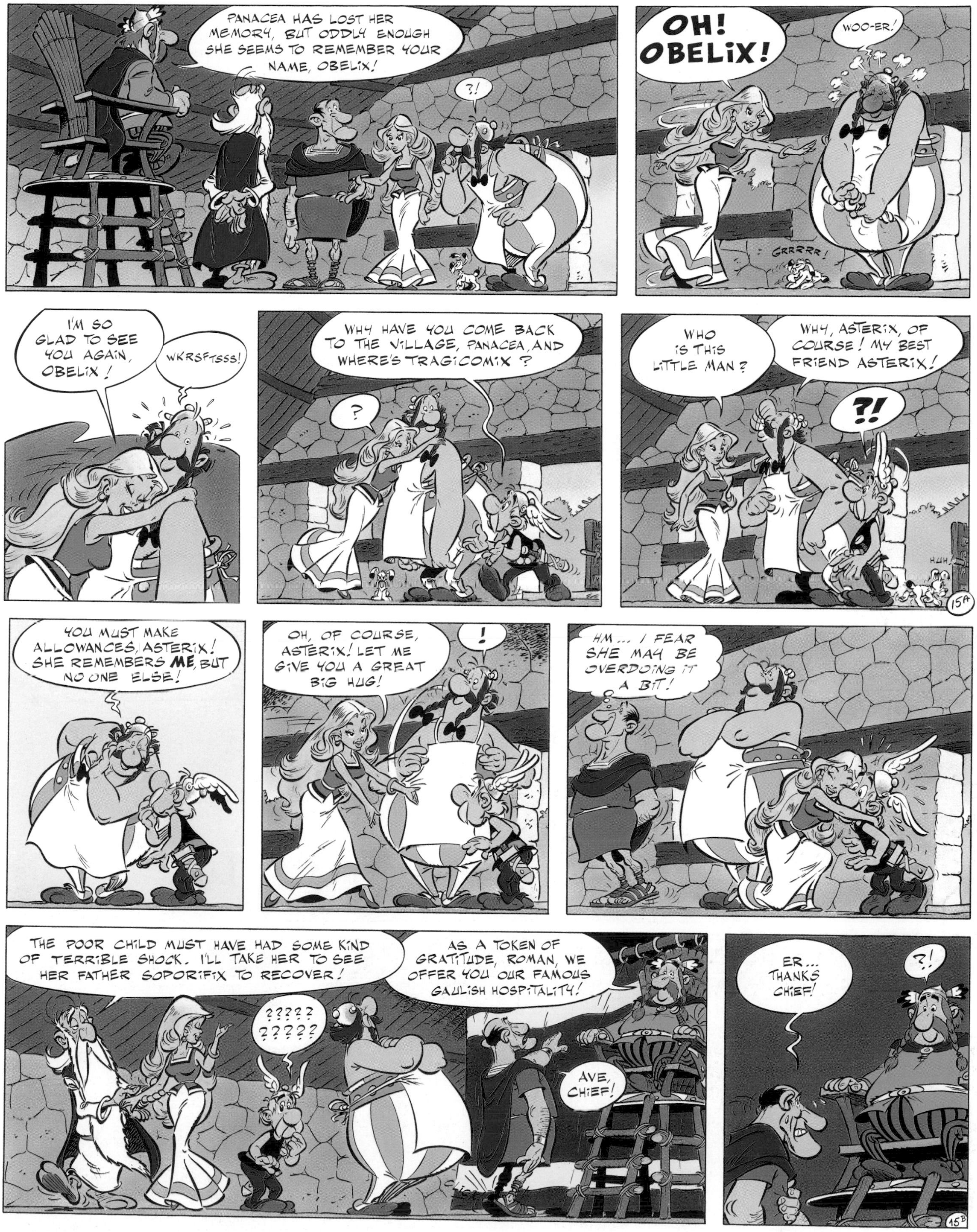
PANACEA HAS LOST HER MEMORY, BUT ODDLY ENOUGH SHE SEEMS TO REMEMBER YOUR NAME, OBELIX!
?!
OH! OBELIX!
WOO-ER!
GRRRRR!
I'M SO GLAD TO SEE YOU AGAIN, OBELIX!
WKRSFTSSS!
WHY HAVE YOU COME BACK TO THE VILLAGE, PANACEA, AND WHERE'S TRAGICOMIX?
?
WHO IS THIS LITTLE MAN?
WHY, ASTERIX, OF COURSE! MY BEST FRIEND ASTERIX!
?!
HUH!
15A
YOU MUST MAKE ALLOWANCES, ASTERIX! SHE REMEMBERS ME, BUT NO ONE ELSE!
OH, OF COURSE, ASTERIX! LET ME GIVE YOU A GREAT BIG HUG!
!
HM... I FEAR SHE MAY BE OVERDOING IT A BIT!
THE POOR CHILD MUST HAVE HAD SOME KIND OF TERRIBLE SHOCK. I'LL TAKE HER TO SEE HER FATHER SOPORIFIX TO RECOVER!
?????
?????
AS A TOKEN OF GRATITUDE, ROMAN, WE OFFER YOU OUR FAMOUS GAULISH HOSPITALITY!
AVE, CHIEF!
ER... THANKS CHIEF!
?!
15B

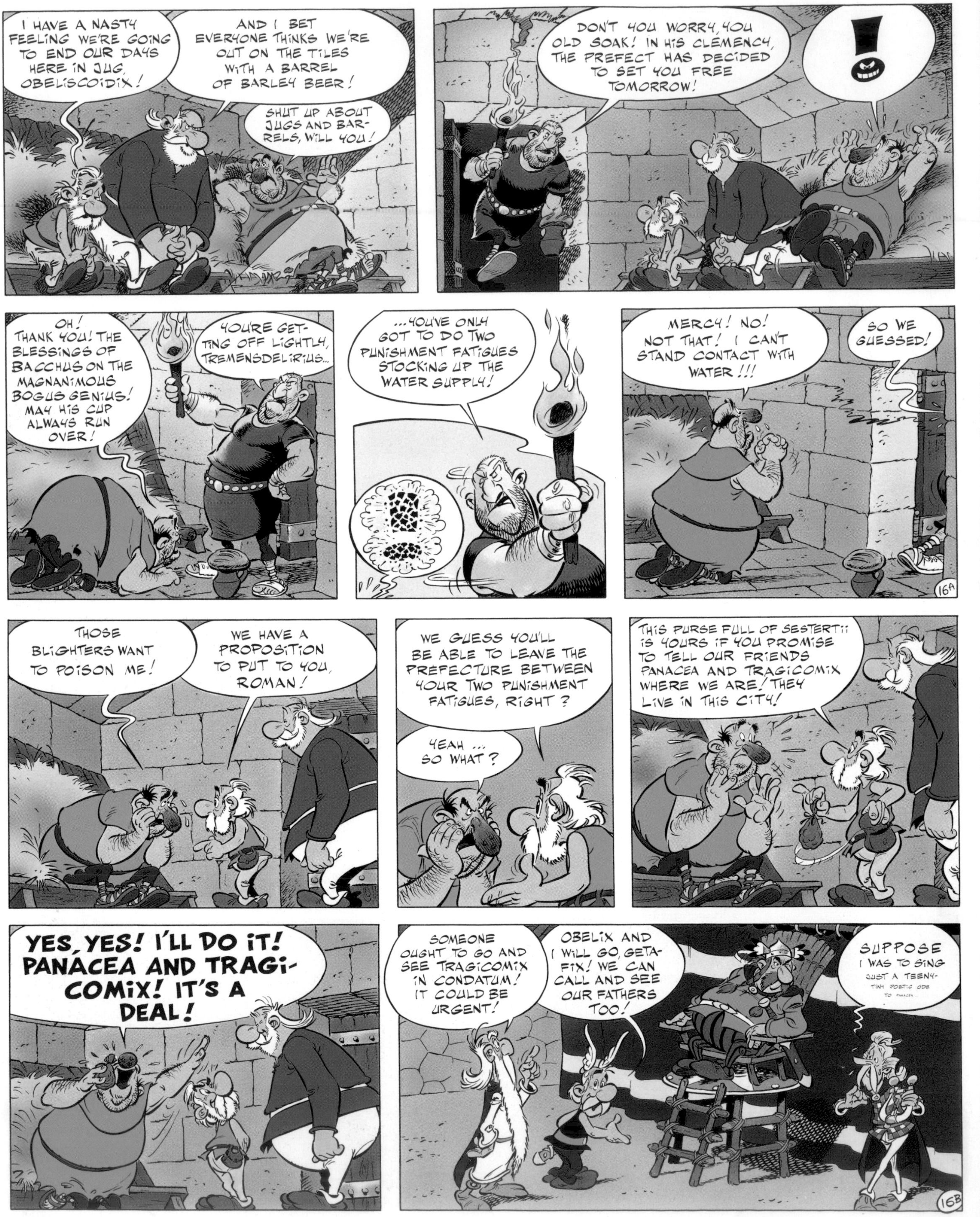
I HAVE A NASTY FEELING WE'RE GOING TO END OUR DAYS HERE IN JUG, OBELISCOIDIX!
AND I BET EVERYONE THINKS WE'RE OUT ON THE TILES WITH A BARREL OF BARLEY BEER!
SHUT UP ABOUT JUGS AND BARRELS, WILL YOU!
DON'T YOU WORRY, YOU OLD SOAK! IN HIS CLÉMENCY, THE PREFECT HAS DECIDED TO SET YOU FREE TOMORROW!
!
OH! THANK YOU! THE BLESSINGS OF BACCHUS ON THE MAGNANIMOUS BOGUS GENIUS! MAY HIS CUP ALWAYS RUN OVER!
YOU'RE GETTING OFF LIGHTLY, TREMENSDELIRIUS...
...YOU'VE ONLY GOT TO DO TWO PUNISHMENT FATIGUES STOCKING UP THE WATER SUPPLY!
!
MERCY! NO! NOT THAT! I CAN'T STAND CONTACT WITH WATER!!!
SO WE GUESSED!
16A
THOSE BLIGHTERS WANT TO POISON ME!
WE HAVE A PROPOSITION TO PUT TO YOU, ROMAN!
WE GUESS YOU'LL BE ABLE TO LEAVE THE PREFECTURE BETWEEN YOUR TWO PUNISHMENT FATIGUES, RIGHT?
YEAH ... SO WHAT?
THIS PURSE FULL OF SESTERTII IS YOURS IF YOU PROMISE TO TELL OUR FRIENDS PANACEA AND TRAGICOMIX WHERE WE ARE! THEY LIVE IN THIS CITY!
YES, YES! I'LL DO IT! PANACEA AND TRAGICOMIX! IT'S A DEAL!
SOMEONE OUGHT TO GO AND SEE TRAGICOMIX IN CONDATUM! IT COULD BE URGENT!
OBELIX AND I WILL GO, GETAFIX! WE CAN CALL AND SEE OUR FATHERS TOO!
SUPPOSE I WAS TO SING JUST A TEENY-TINY POETIC ODE TO
16B

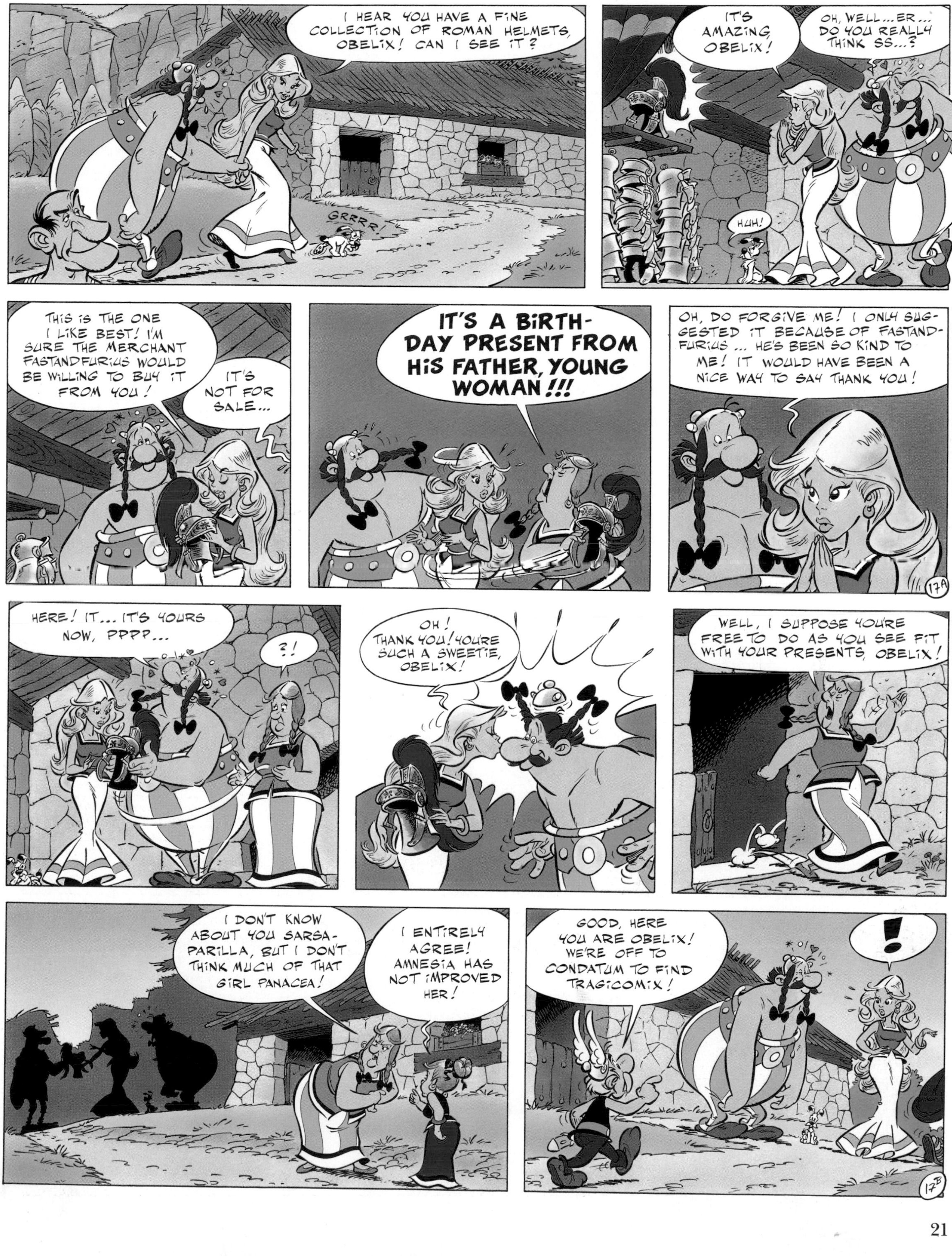
I HEAR YOU HAVE A FINE COLLECTION OF ROMAN HELMETS, OBELIX! CAN I SEE IT?
GRRRR!
IT'S AMAZING, OBELIX!
OH, WELL... ER... DO YOU REALLY THINK SS...?
HUH!
THIS IS THE ONE I LIKE BEST! I'M SURE THE MERCHANT FASTANDFURIUS WOULD BE WILLING TO BUY IT FROM YOU!
IT'S NOT FOR SALE...
IT'S A BIRTH-DAY PRESENT FROM HIS FATHER, YOUNG WOMAN!!!
OH, DO FORGIVE ME! I ONLY SUG-GESTED IT BECAUSE OF FASTAND-FURIUS... HE'S BEEN SO KIND TO ME! IT WOULD HAVE BEEN A NICE WAY TO SAY THANK YOU!
17A
HERE! IT... IT'S YOURS NOW, PPPP...
?!
OH! THANK YOU! YOU'RE SUCH A SWEETIE, OBELIX!
WELL, I SUPPOSE YOU'RE FREE TO DO AS YOU SEE FIT WITH YOUR PRESENTS, OBELIX!
I DON'T KNOW ABOUT YOU SARSA-PARILLA, BUT I DON'T THINK MUCH OF THAT GIRL PANACEA!
I ENTIRELY AGREE! AMNESIA HAS NOT IMPROVED HER!
GOOD, HERE YOU ARE OBELIX! WE'RE OFF TO CONDATUM TO FIND TRAGICOMIX!
!
17B

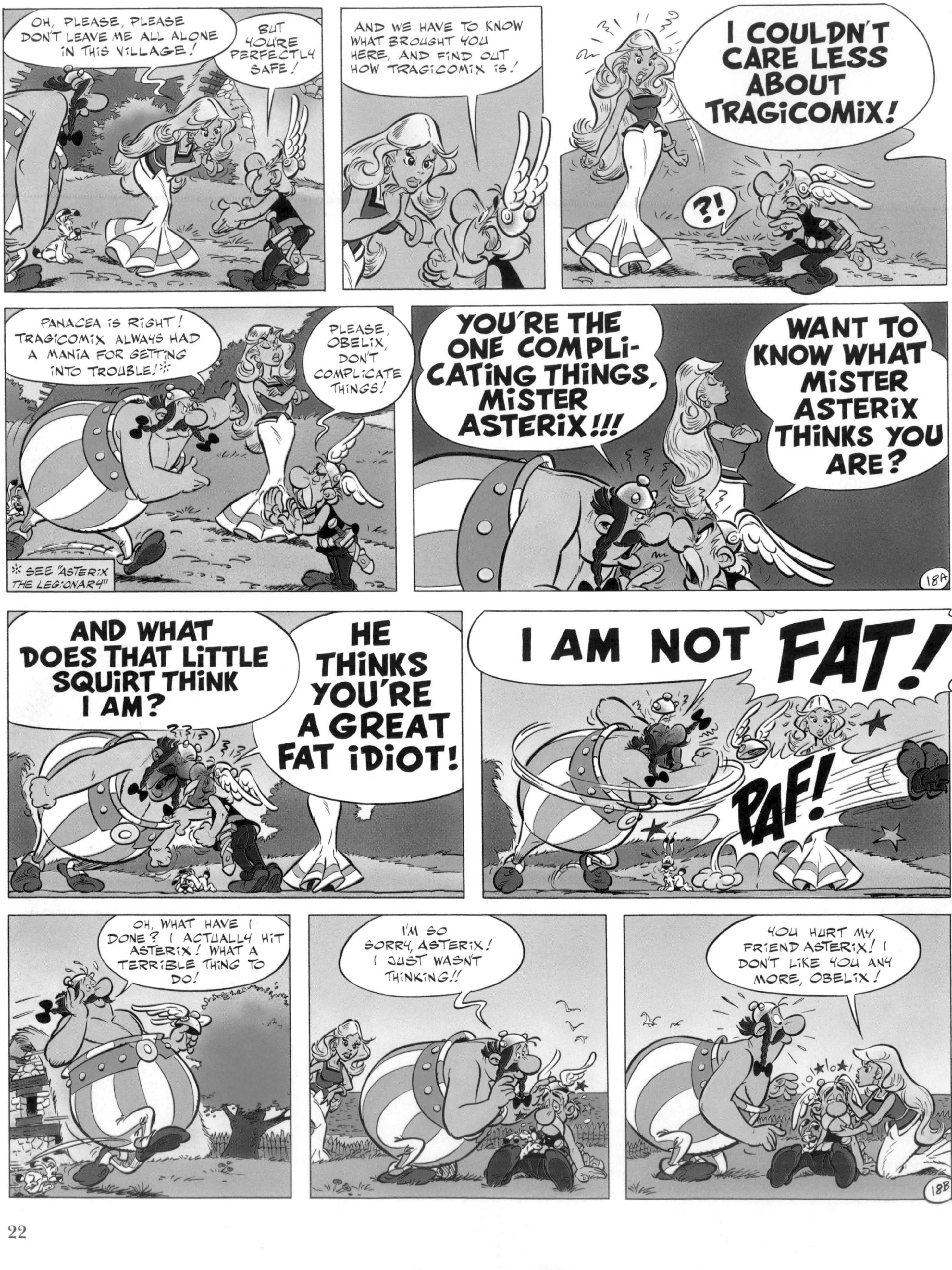

OH, PLEASE, PLEASE DON'T LEAVE ME ALL ALONE IN THIS VILLAGE!
BUT YOU'RE PERFECTLY SAFE!
AND WE HAVE TO KNOW WHAT BROUGHT YOU HERE, AND FIND OUT HOW TRAGICOMIX IS!
I COULDN'T CARE LESS ABOUT TRAGICOMIX!
?!
PANACEA IS RIGHT! TRAGICOMIX ALWAYS HAD A MANIA FOR GETTING INTO TROUBLE!*
PLEASE, OBELIX, DON'T COMPLICATE THINGS!
* SEE "ASTERIX THE LEGIONARY"
YOU'RE THE ONE COMPLICATING THINGS, MISTER ASTERIX!!!
WANT TO KNOW WHAT MISTER ASTERIX THINKS YOU ARE?
18A
AND WHAT DOES THAT LITTLE SQUIRT THINK I AM?
HE THINKS YOU'RE A GREAT FAT IDIOT!
I AM NOT FAT!
PAF!
OH, WHAT HAVE I DONE? I ACTUALLY HIT ASTERIX! WHAT A TERRIBLE THING TO DO!
I'M SO SORRY, ASTERIX! I JUST WASN'T THINKING!!
YOU HURT MY FRIEND ASTERIX! I DON'T LIKE YOU ANY MORE, OBELIX!
18B

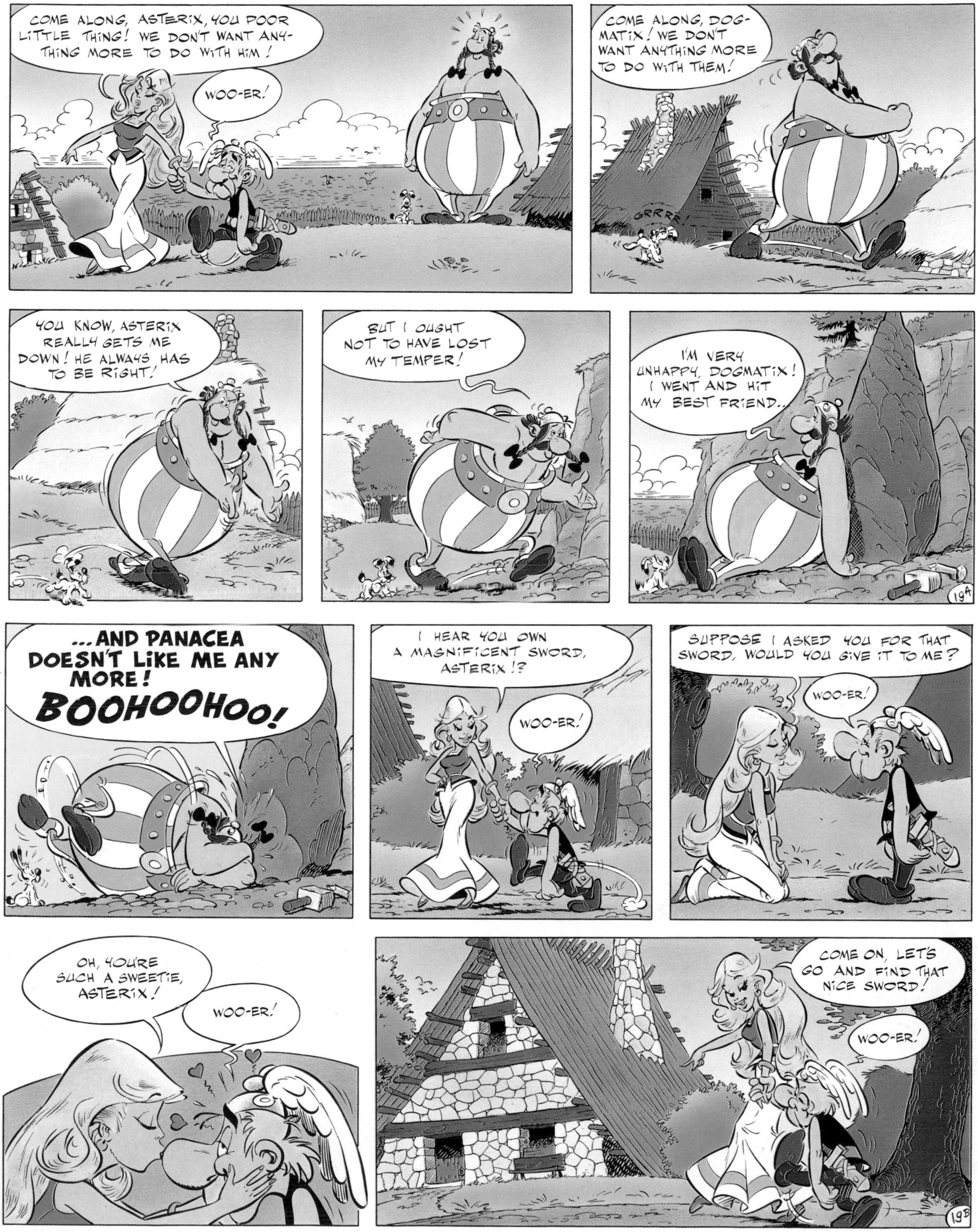
COME ALONG, ASTERIX, YOU POOR LITTLE THING! WE DON'T WANT ANYTHING MORE TO DO WITH HIM!
WOO-ER!
COME ALONG, DOGMATIX! WE DON'T WANT ANYTHING MORE TO DO WITH THEM!
GRRRR!
YOU KNOW, ASTERIX REALLY GETS ME DOWN! HE ALWAYS HAS TO BE RIGHT!
BUT I OUGHT NOT TO HAVE LOST MY TEMPER!
I'M VERY UNHAPPY, DOGMATIX! I WENT AND HIT MY BEST FRIEND...
...AND PANACEA DOESN'T LIKE ME ANY MORE! BOOHOOHOO!
I HEAR YOU OWN A MAGNIFICENT SWORD, ASTERIX!?
WOO-ER!
SUPPOSE I ASKED YOU FOR THAT SWORD, WOULD YOU GIVE IT TO ME?
WOO-ER!
OH, YOU'RE SUCH A SWEETIE, ASTERIX!
WOO-ER!
COME ON, LET'S GO AND FIND THAT NICE SWORD!
WOO-ER!

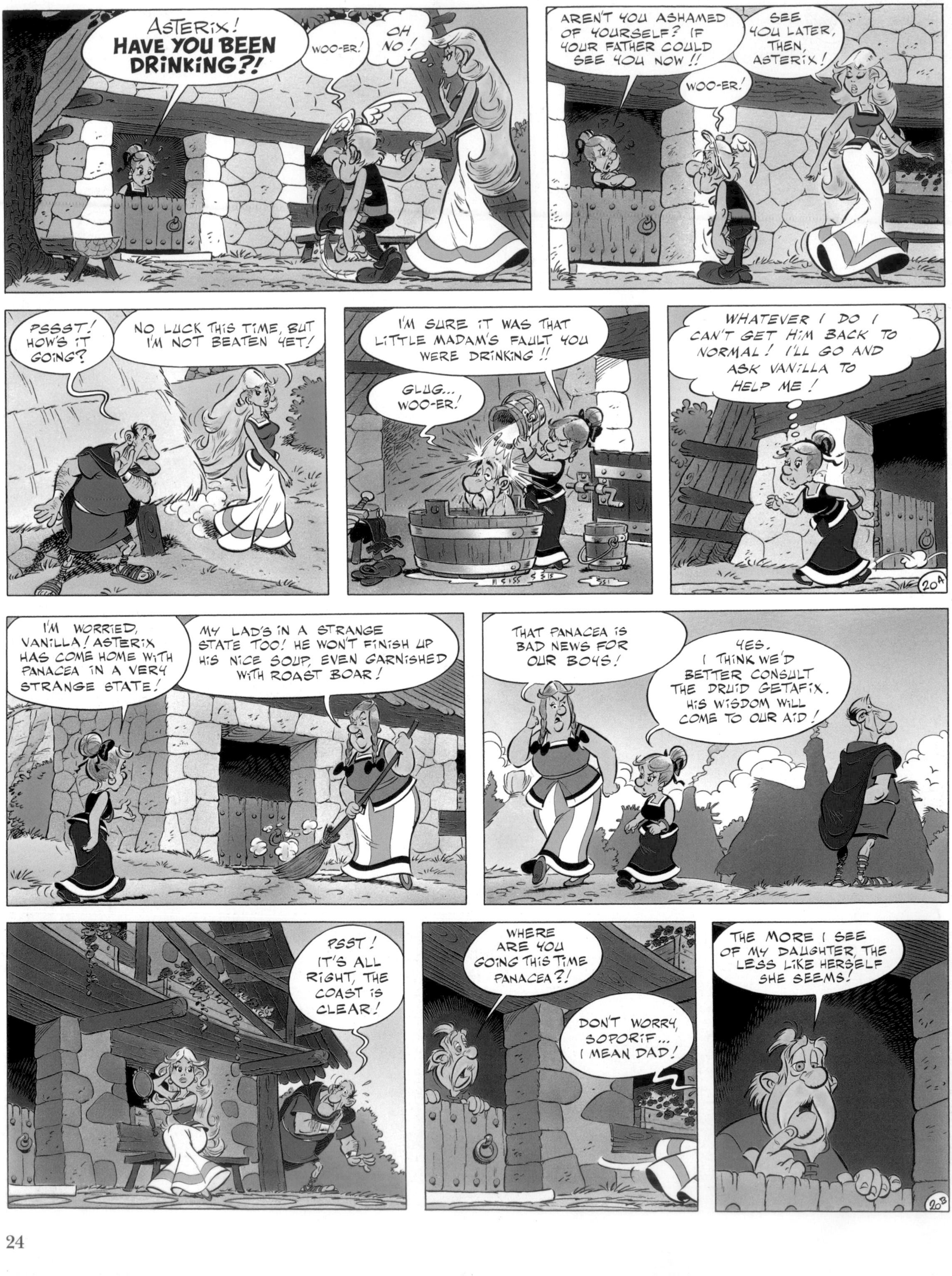

ASTERIX! HAVE YOU BEEN DRINKING?!
WOO-ER!
OH NO!
AREN'T YOU ASHAMED OF YOURSELF? IF YOUR FATHER COULD SEE YOU NOW!!
WOO-ER!
SEE YOU LATER, THEN, ASTERIX!
PSSST! HOW'S IT GOING?
NO LUCK THIS TIME, BUT I'M NOT BEATEN YET!
I'M SURE IT WAS THAT LITTLE MADAM'S FAULT YOU WERE DRINKING!!
GLUG... WOO-ER!
WHATEVER I DO I CAN'T GET HIM BACK TO NORMAL! I'LL GO AND ASK VANILLA TO HELP ME!
20A
I'M WORRIED, VANILLA! ASTERIX HAS COME HOME WITH PANACEA IN A VERY STRANGE STATE!
MY LAD'S IN A STRANGE STATE TOO! HE WON'T FINISH UP HIS NICE SOUP, EVEN GARNISHED WITH ROAST BOAR!
THAT PANACEA IS BAD NEWS FOR OUR BOYS!
YES. I THINK WE'D BETTER CONSULT THE DRUID GETAFIX. HIS WISDOM WILL COME TO OUR AID!
PSST! IT'S ALL RIGHT, THE COAST IS CLEAR!
WHERE ARE YOU GOING THIS TIME PANACEA?!
DON'T WORRY, SOPORIF... I MEAN DAD!
THE MORE I SEE OF MY DAUGHTER, THE LESS LIKE HERSELF SHE SEEMS!
20B

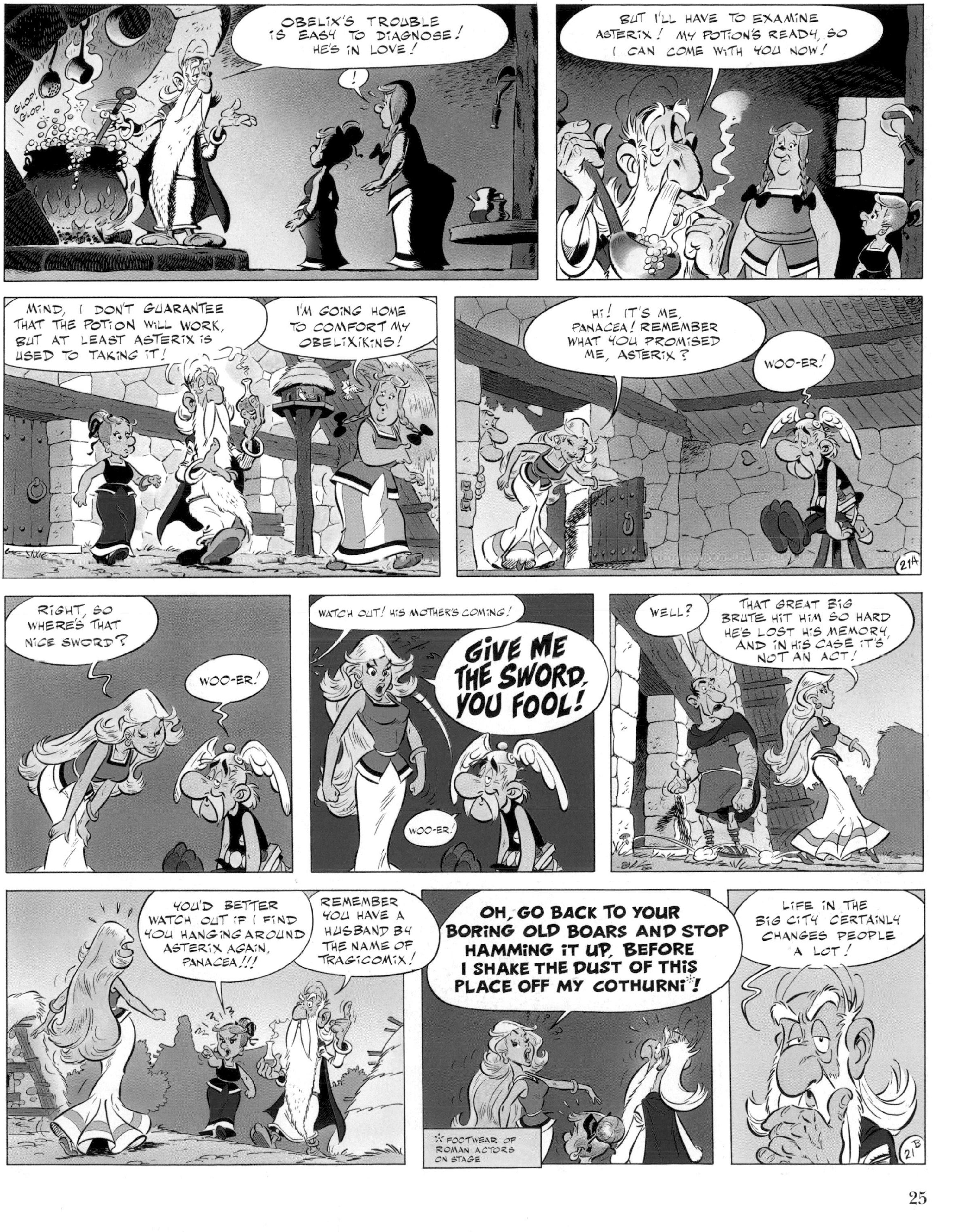
GLOP! GLOP!
OBELIX'S TROUBLE IS EASY TO DIAGNOSE! HE'S IN LOVE!
!
BUT I'LL HAVE TO EXAMINE ASTERIX! MY POTION'S READY, SO I CAN COME WITH YOU NOW!
MIND, I DON'T GUARANTEE THAT THE POTION WILL WORK, BUT AT LEAST ASTERIX IS USED TO TAKING IT!
I'M GOING HOME TO COMFORT MY OBELIXIKINS!
HI! IT'S ME, PANACEA! REMEMBER WHAT YOU PROMISED ME, ASTERIX?
WOO-ER!
21A
RIGHT, SO WHERE'S THAT NICE SWORD?
WOO-ER!
WATCH OUT! HIS MOTHER'S COMING!
GIVE ME THE SWORD, YOU FOOL!
WOO-ER!
WELL?
THAT GREAT BIG BRUTE HIT HIM SO HARD HE'S LOST HIS MEMORY, AND IN HIS CASE IT'S NOT AN ACT!
YOU'D BETTER WATCH OUT IF I FIND YOU HANGING AROUND ASTERIX AGAIN, PANACEA!!!
REMEMBER YOU HAVE A HUSBAND BY THE NAME OF TRAGICOMIX!
OH, GO BACK TO YOUR BORING OLD BOARS AND STOP HAMMING IT UP, BEFORE I SHAKE THE DUST OF THIS PLACE OFF MY COTHURNI*!
* FOOTWEAR OF ROMAN ACTORS ON STAGE
LIFE IN THE BIG CITY CERTAINLY CHANGES PEOPLE A LOT!
21B

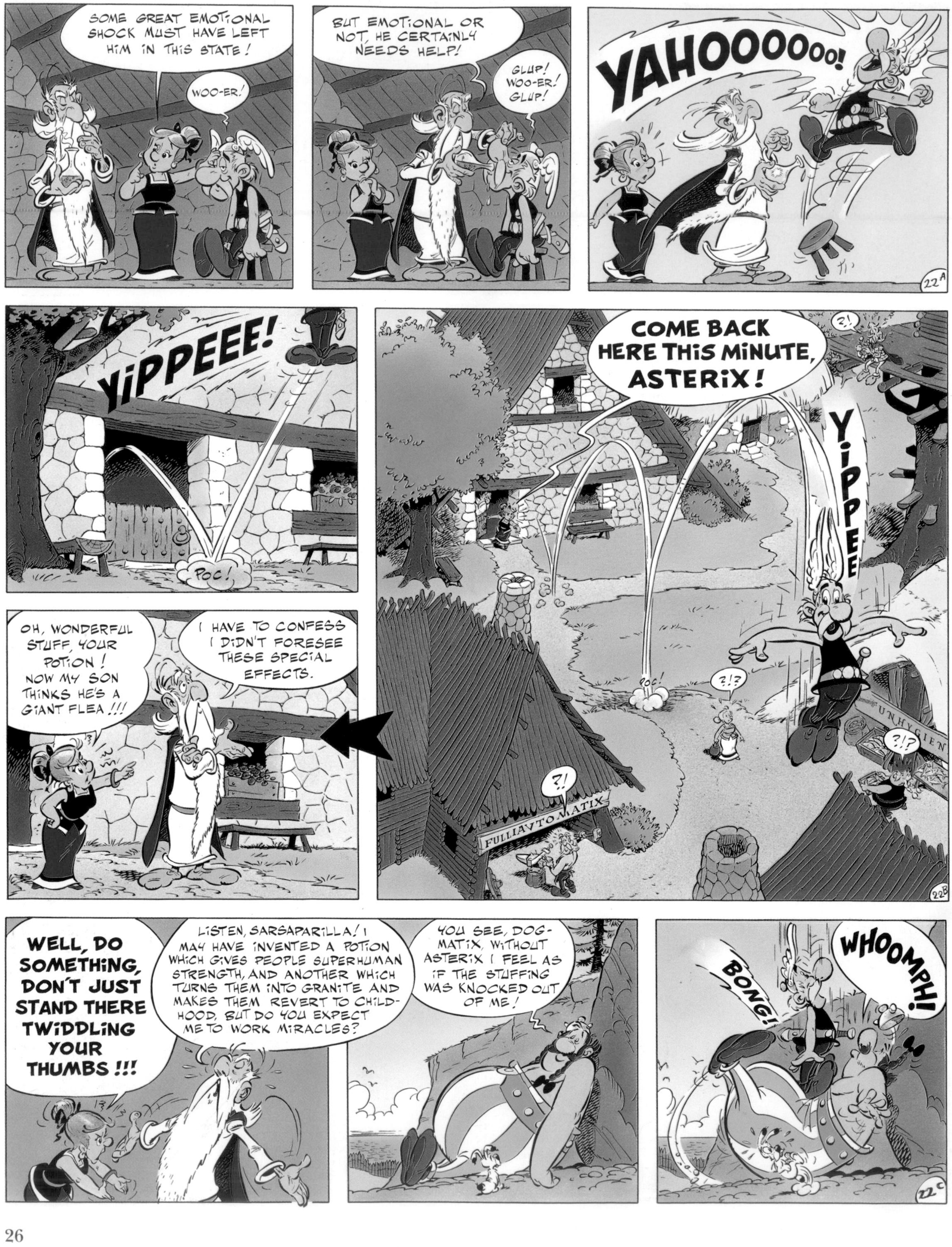
SOME GREAT EMOTIONAL SHOCK MUST HAVE LEFT HIM IN THIS STATE!
WOO-ER!
BUT EMOTIONAL OR NOT, HE CERTAINLY NEEDS HELP!
GLUP! WOO-ER! GLUP!
YAHOOOOOO!
YIPPEEE!
POC!
COME BACK HERE THIS MINUTE, ASTERIX!
YIPPEE
POC!
?!
?!?
?!?
?!
FULLIAVTOMATIX
UNHYGIEN
OH, WONDERFUL STUFF, YOUR POTION! NOW MY SON THINKS HE'S A GIANT FLEA!!!
I HAVE TO CONFESS I DIDN'T FORESEE THESE SPECIAL EFFECTS.
WELL, DO SOMETHING, DON'T JUST STAND THERE TWIDDLING YOUR THUMBS!!!
LISTEN, SARSAPARILLA! I MAY HAVE INVENTED A POTION WHICH GIVES PEOPLE SUPERHUMAN STRENGTH, AND ANOTHER WHICH TURNS THEM INTO GRANITE AND MAKES THEM REVERT TO CHILDHOOD, BUT DO YOU EXPECT ME TO WORK MIRACLES?
YOU SEE, DOGMATIX, WITHOUT ASTERIX I FEEL AS IF THE STUFFING WAS KNOCKED OUT OF ME!
BONG!
WHOOMPH!

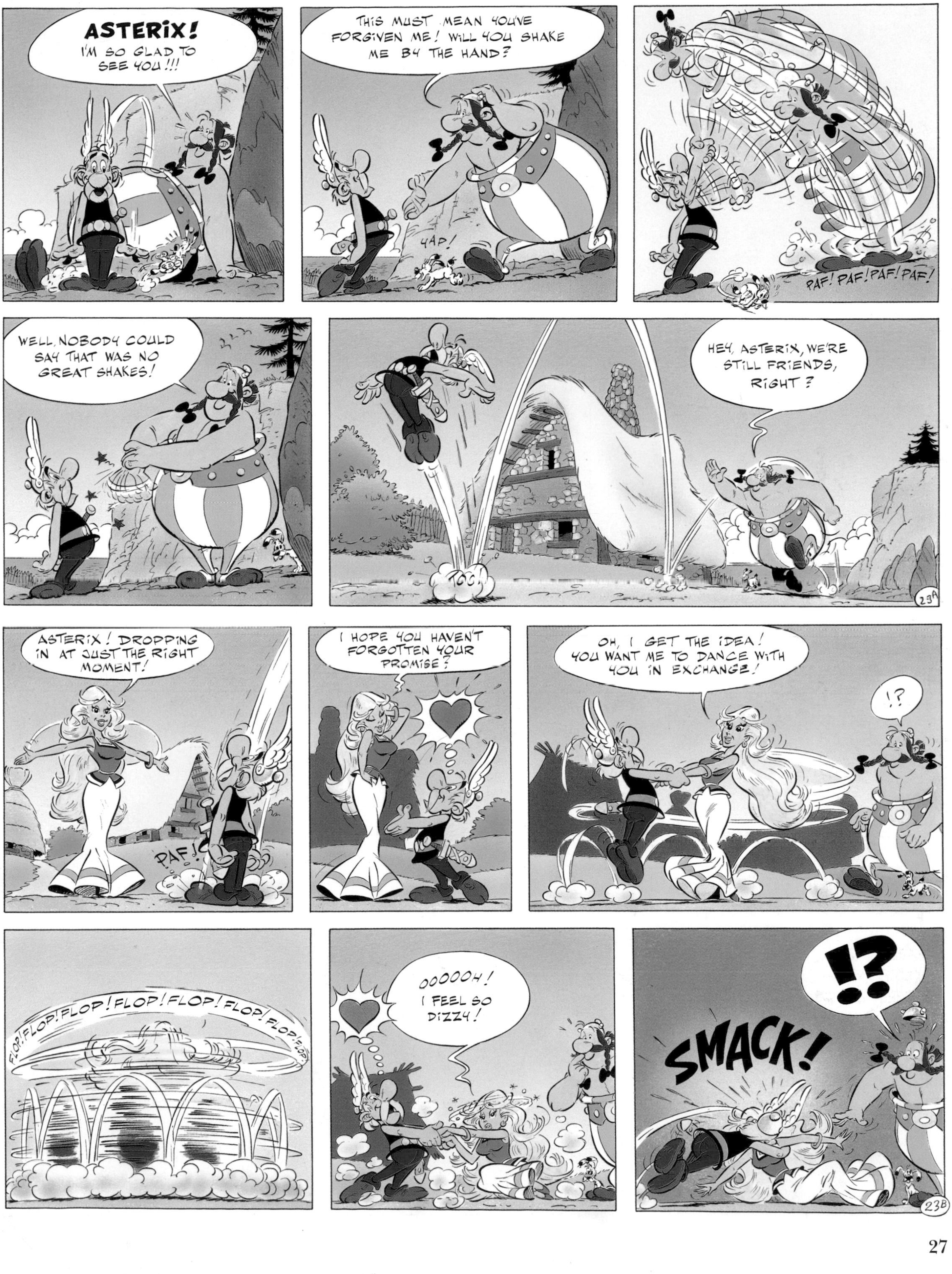
ASTERIX! I'M SO GLAD TO SEE YOU!!!
THIS MUST MEAN YOU'VE FORGIVEN ME! WILL YOU SHAKE ME BY THE HAND?
YAP!
PAF! PAF! PAF! PAF!
WELL, NOBODY COULD SAY THAT WAS NO GREAT SHAKES!
HEY, ASTERIX, WE'RE STILL FRIENDS, RIGHT?
ASTERIX! DROPPING IN AT JUST THE RIGHT MOMENT!
PAF!
I HOPE YOU HAVEN'T FORGOTTEN YOUR PROMISE?
OH, I GET THE IDEA! YOU WANT ME TO DANCE WITH YOU IN EXCHANGE!
!?
FLOP! FLOP! FLOP! FLOP! FLOP! FLOP! FLOP!
OOOOOH! I FEEL SO DIZZY!
!?
SMACK!

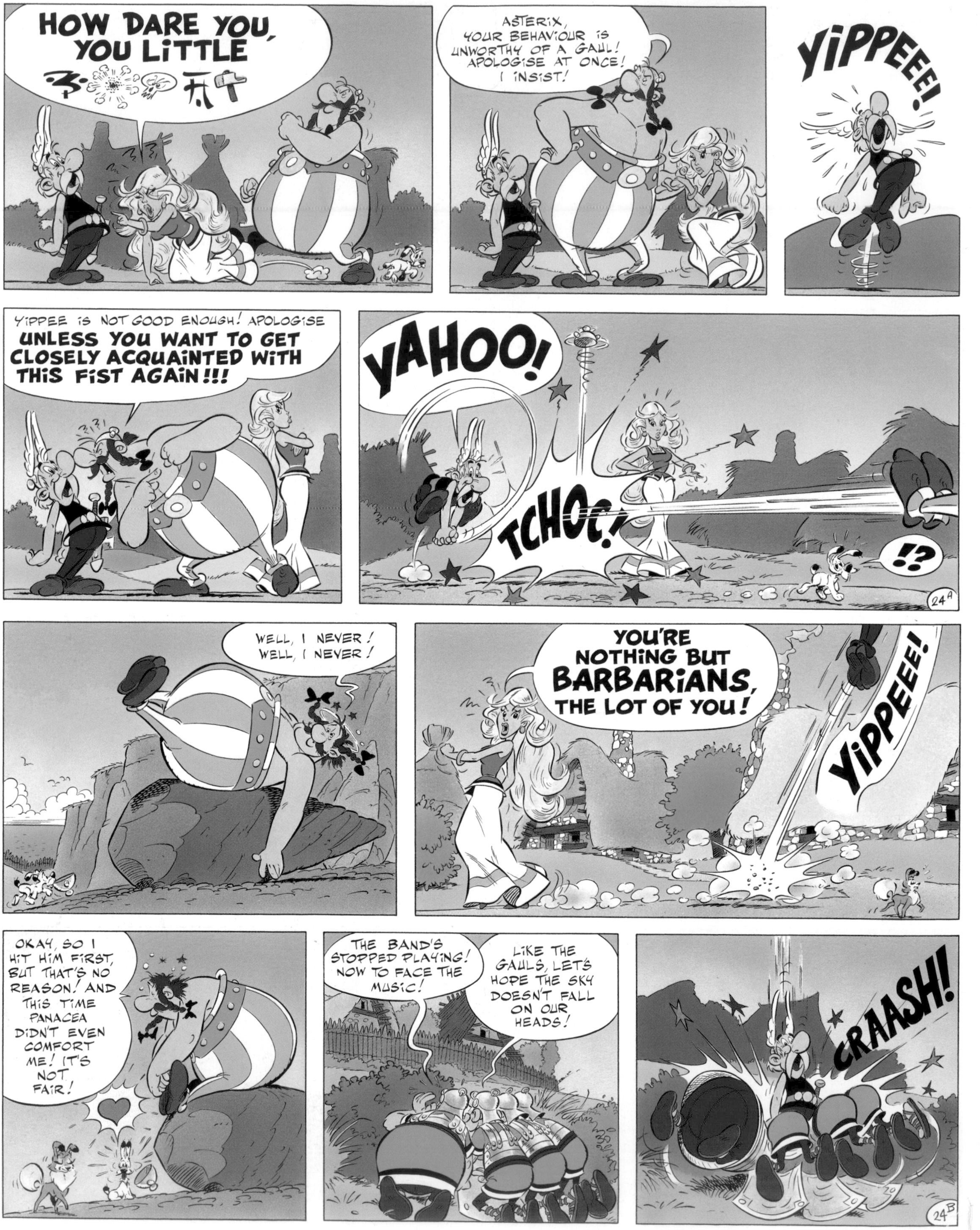
HOW DARE YOU, YOU LITTLE
ASTERIX, YOUR BEHAVIOUR IS UNWORTHY OF A GAUL! APOLOGISE AT ONCE! I INSIST!
YIPPEEE!
YIPPEE IS NOT GOOD ENOUGH! APOLOGISE UNLESS YOU WANT TO GET CLOSELY ACQUAINTED WITH THIS FIST AGAIN!!!
YAHOO!
TCHOC!
!?
24A
WELL, I NEVER! WELL, I NEVER!
YOU'RE NOTHING BUT BARBARIANS, THE LOT OF YOU!
YIPPEEE!
OKAY, SO I HIT HIM FIRST, BUT THAT'S NO REASON! AND THIS TIME PANACEA DIDN'T EVEN COMFORT ME! IT'S NOT FAIR!
THE BAND'S STOPPED PLAYING! NOW TO FACE THE MUSIC!
LIKE THE GAULS, LET'S HOPE THE SKY DOESN'T FALL ON OUR HEADS!
CRAASH!
24B

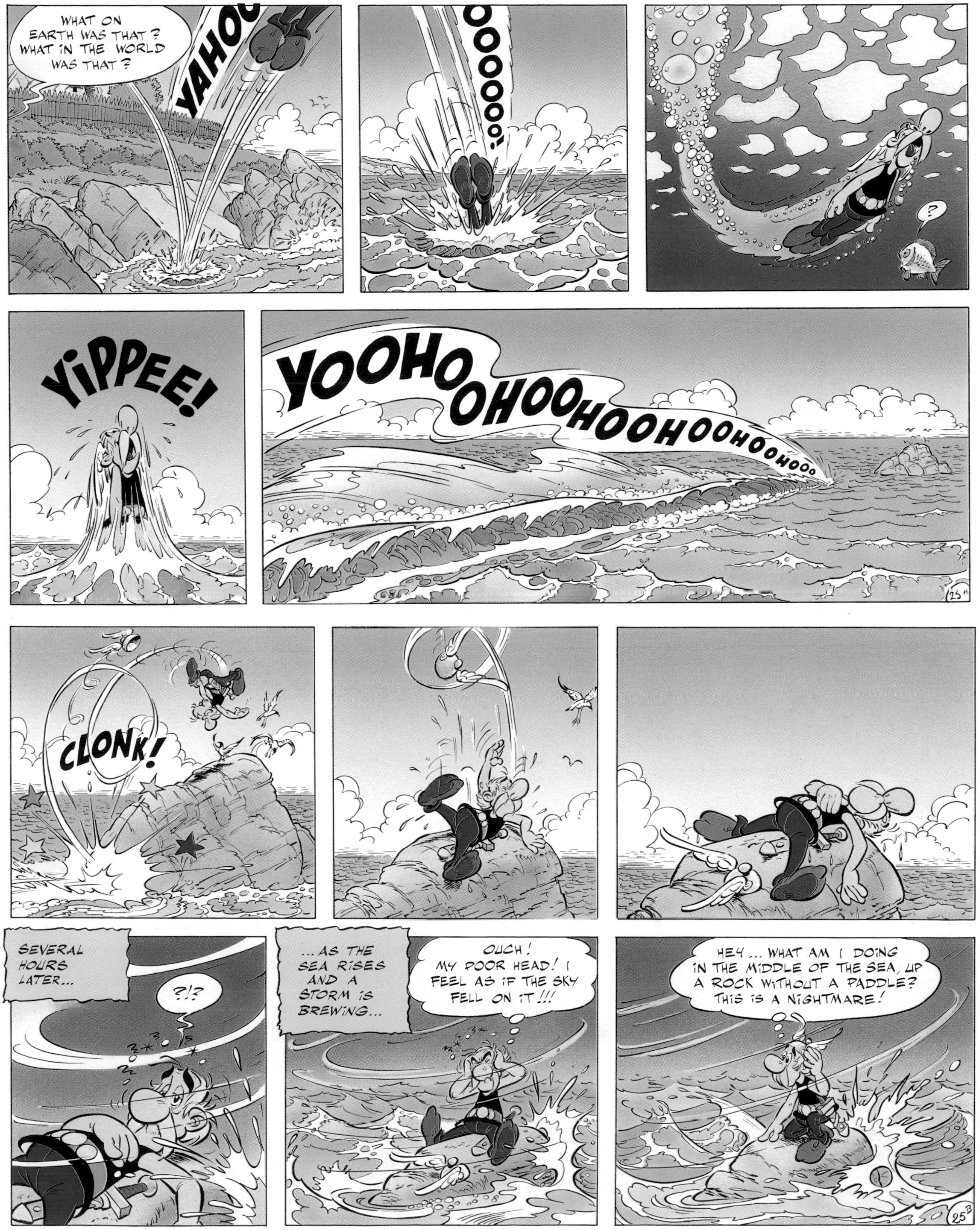
WHAT ON EARTH WAS THAT ? WHAT IN THE WORLD WAS THAT ?
YAHOO
OOOOOO
YIPPEE!
YOOHOOHOOHOOHOOHOOhOOhOOO
CLONK!
SEVERAL HOURS LATER...
?!?
...AS THE SEA RISES AND A STORM IS BREWING...
OUCH! MY POOR HEAD! I FEEL AS IF THE SKY FELL ON IT!!!
HEY ... WHAT AM I DOING IN THE MIDDLE OF THE SEA, UP A ROCK WITHOUT A PADDLE? THIS IS A NIGHTMARE!

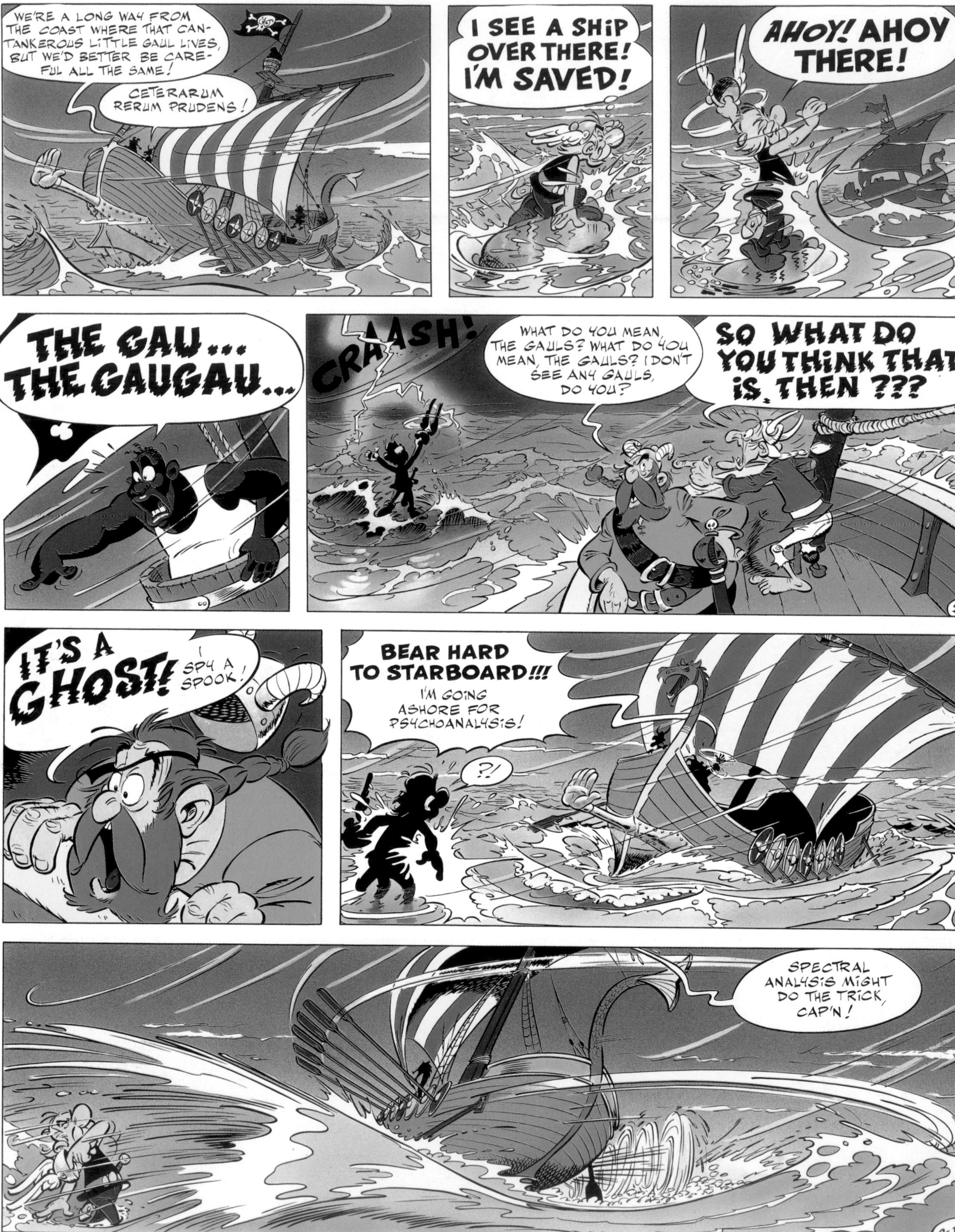
WE'RE A LONG WAY FROM THE COAST WHERE THAT CANTANKEROUS LITTLE GAUL LIVES, BUT WE'D BETTER BE CAREFUL ALL THE SAME!
CETERARUM RERUM PRUDENS!
I SEE A SHIP OVER THERE! I'M SAVED!
AHOY! AHOY THERE!
THE GAU... THE GAUGAU...
CRAASH!
WHAT DO YOU MEAN, THE GAULS? WHAT DO YOU MEAN, THE GAULS? I DON'T SEE ANY GAULS, DO YOU?
SO WHAT DO YOU THINK THAT IS, THEN ???
26A
IT'S A GHOST!
I SPY A SPOOK!
BEAR HARD TO STARBOARD!!!
I'M GOING ASHORE FOR PSYCHOANALYSIS!
?!
SPECTRAL ANALYSIS MIGHT DO THE TRICK, CAP'N!
26B

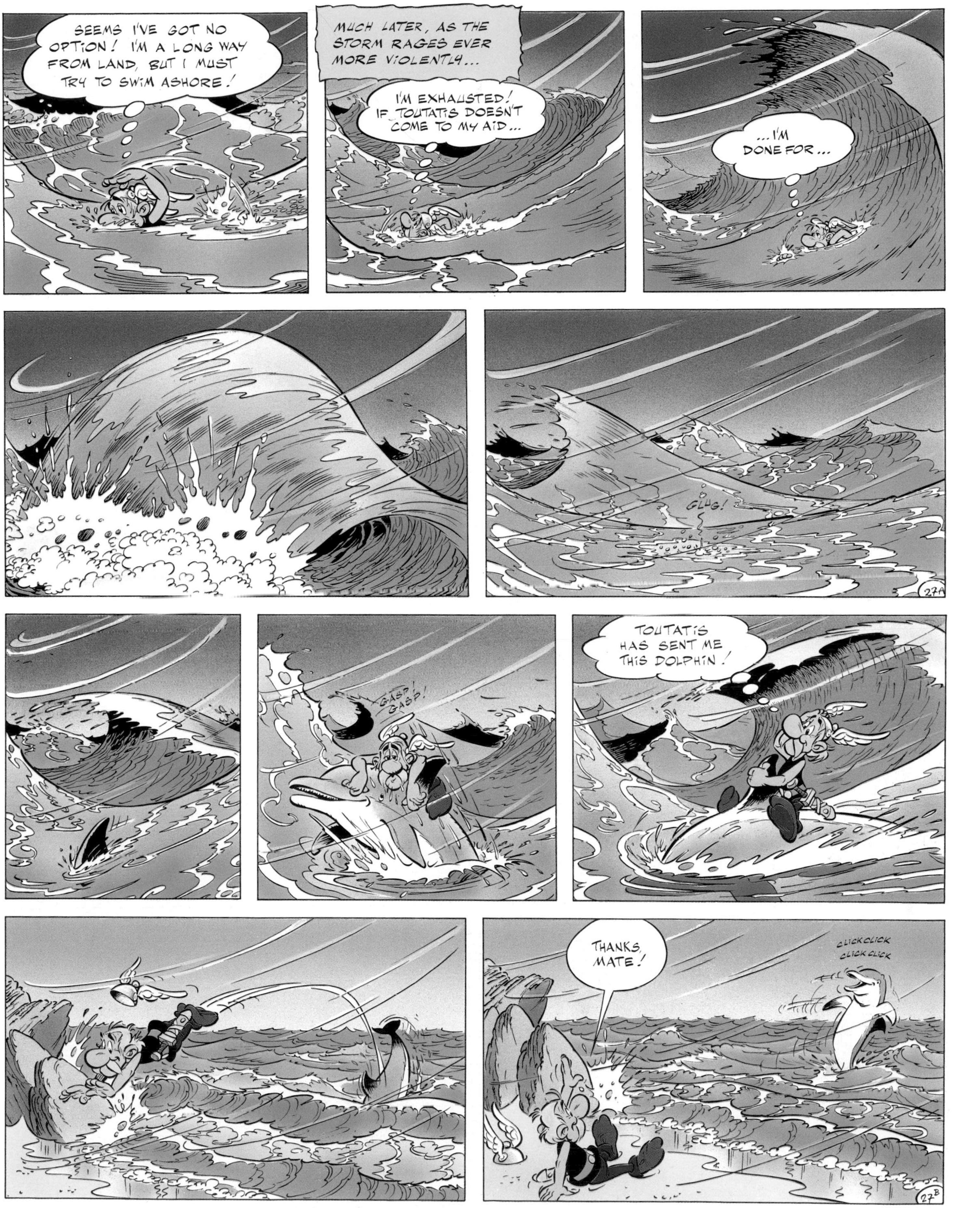
SEEMS I'VE GOT NO OPTION! I'M A LONG WAY FROM LAND, BUT I MUST TRY TO SWIM ASHORE!
MUCH LATER, AS THE STORM RAGES EVER MORE VIOLENTLY...
I'M EXHAUSTED! IF TOUTATIS DOESN'T COME TO MY AID...
...I'M DONE FOR...
GLUG!
GASP! GASP!
TOUTATIS HAS SENT ME THIS DOLPHIN!
THANKS, MATE!
CLICK CLICK
CLICK CLICK

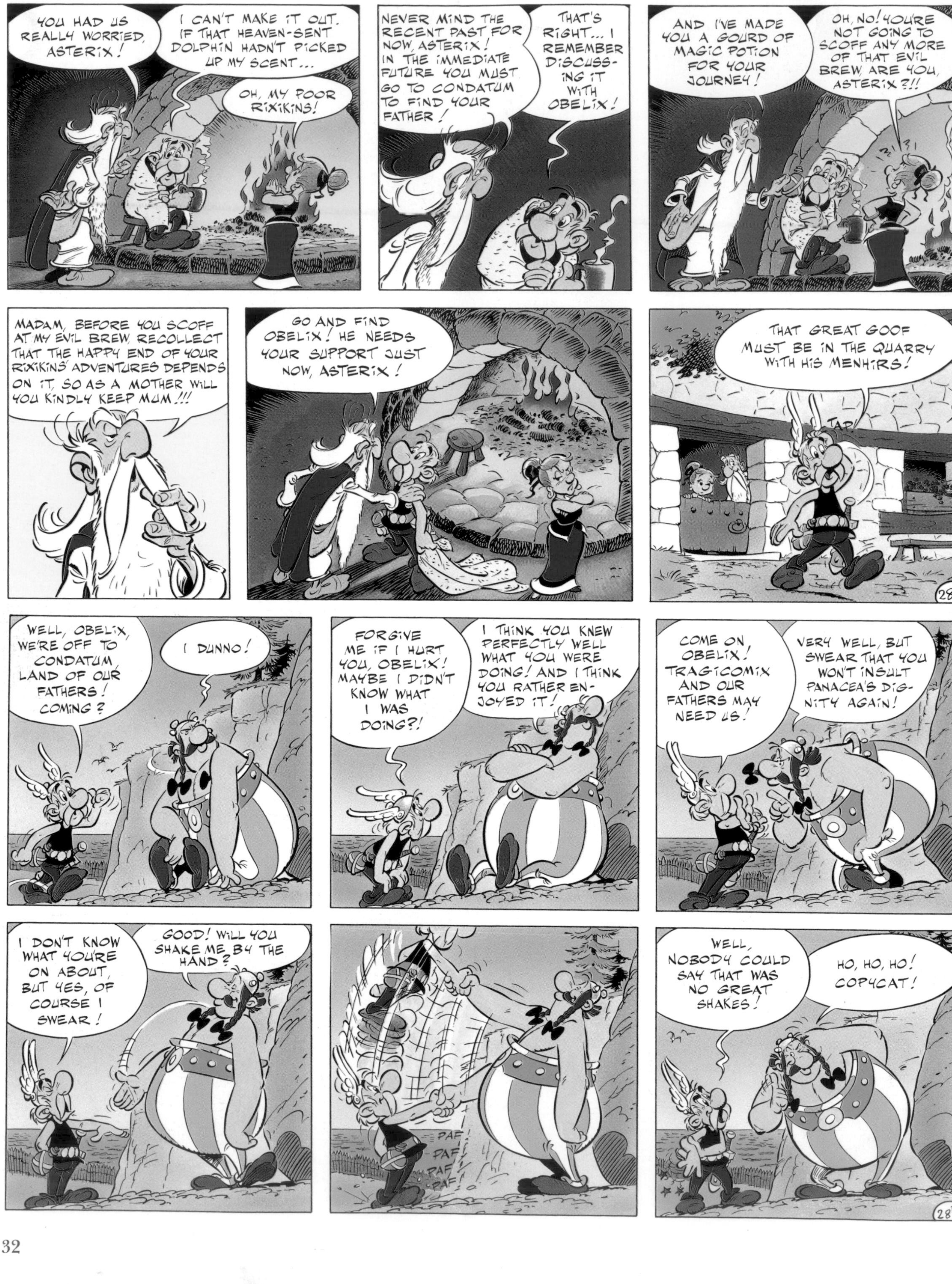

YOU HAD US REALLY WORRIED, ASTERIX!
I CAN'T MAKE IT OUT. IF THAT HEAVEN-SENT DOLPHIN HADN'T PICKED UP MY SCENT...
OH, MY POOR RIXIKINS!
NEVER MIND THE RECENT PAST FOR NOW, ASTERIX! IN THE IMMEDIATE FUTURE YOU MUST GO TO CONDATUM TO FIND YOUR FATHER!
THAT'S RIGHT... I REMEMBER DISCUSSING IT WITH OBELIX!
AND I'VE MADE YOU A GOURD OF MAGIC POTION FOR YOUR JOURNEY!
OH, NO! YOU'RE NOT GOING TO SCOFF ANY MORE OF THAT EVIL BREW, ARE YOU, ASTERIX?!!
MADAM, BEFORE YOU SCOFF AT MY EVIL BREW, RECOLLECT THAT THE HAPPY END OF YOUR RIXIKINS' ADVENTURES DEPENDS ON IT, SO AS A MOTHER WILL YOU KINDLY KEEP MUM!!!
GO AND FIND OBELIX! HE NEEDS YOUR SUPPORT JUST NOW, ASTERIX!
THAT GREAT GOOF MUST BE IN THE QUARRY WITH HIS MENHIRS!
TAP
28A
WELL, OBELIX, WE'RE OFF TO CONDATUM, LAND OF OUR FATHERS! COMING?
I DUNNO!
FORGIVE ME IF I HURT YOU, OBELIX! MAYBE I DIDN'T KNOW WHAT I WAS DOING?!
I THINK YOU KNEW PERFECTLY WELL WHAT YOU WERE DOING! AND I THINK YOU RATHER ENJOYED IT!
COME ON, OBELIX! TRAGICOMIX AND OUR FATHERS MAY NEED US!
VERY WELL, BUT SWEAR THAT YOU WON'T INSULT PANACEA'S DIGNITY AGAIN!
I DON'T KNOW WHAT YOU'RE ON ABOUT, BUT YES, OF COURSE! SWEAR!
GOOD! WILL YOU SHAKE ME BY THE HAND?
PAF! PAF! PAF! PAF!
WELL, NOBODY COULD SAY THAT WAS NO GREAT SHAKES!
HO, HO, HO! COPYCAT!
28B

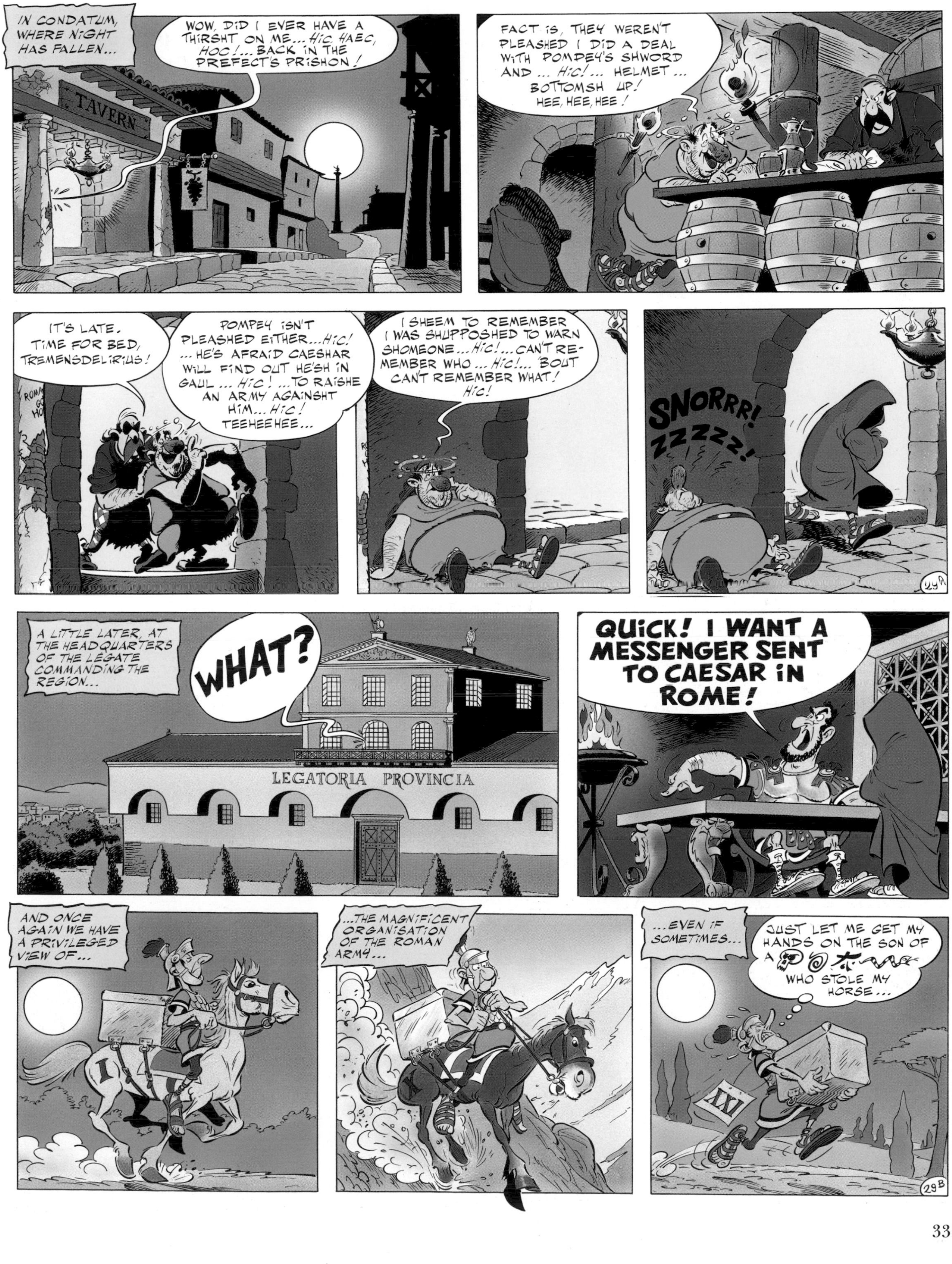
IN CONDATUM, WHERE NIGHT HAS FALLEN...
WOW, DID I EVER HAVE A THIRSHT ON ME... HIC, HAEC, HOC!... BACK IN THE PREFECT'S PRISHON!
TAVERN
FACT IS, THEY WEREN'T PLEASHED I DID A DEAL WITH POMPEY'S SHWORD AND ... HIC!... HELMET... BOTTOMSH UP! HEE, HEE, HEE!
IT'S LATE. TIME FOR BED, TREMENSDELIRIUS!
POMPEY ISN'T PLEASHED EITHER...HIC! ... HE'S AFRAID CAESHAR WILL FIND OUT HE'SH IN GAUL ... HIC! ...TO RAISHE AN ARMY AGAINSHT HIM... HIC! TEEHEEHEE...
I SHEEM TO REMEMBER I WAS SHUPPOSHED TO WARN SHOMEONE...HIC!...CAN'T REMEMBER WHO ... HIC!... 'BOUT CAN'T REMEMBER WHAT! HIC!
SNORRR! ZZZZZ!
A LITTLE LATER, AT THE HEADQUARTERS OF THE LEGATE COMMANDING THE REGION...
WHAT?
LEGATORIA PROVINCIA
QUICK! I WANT A MESSENGER SENT TO CAESAR IN ROME!
AND ONCE AGAIN WE HAVE A PRIVILEGED VIEW OF...
...THE MAGNIFICENT ORGANISATION OF THE ROMAN ARMY...
...EVEN IF SOMETIMES...
JUST LET ME GET MY HANDS ON THE SON OF A ... WHO STOLE MY HORSE...

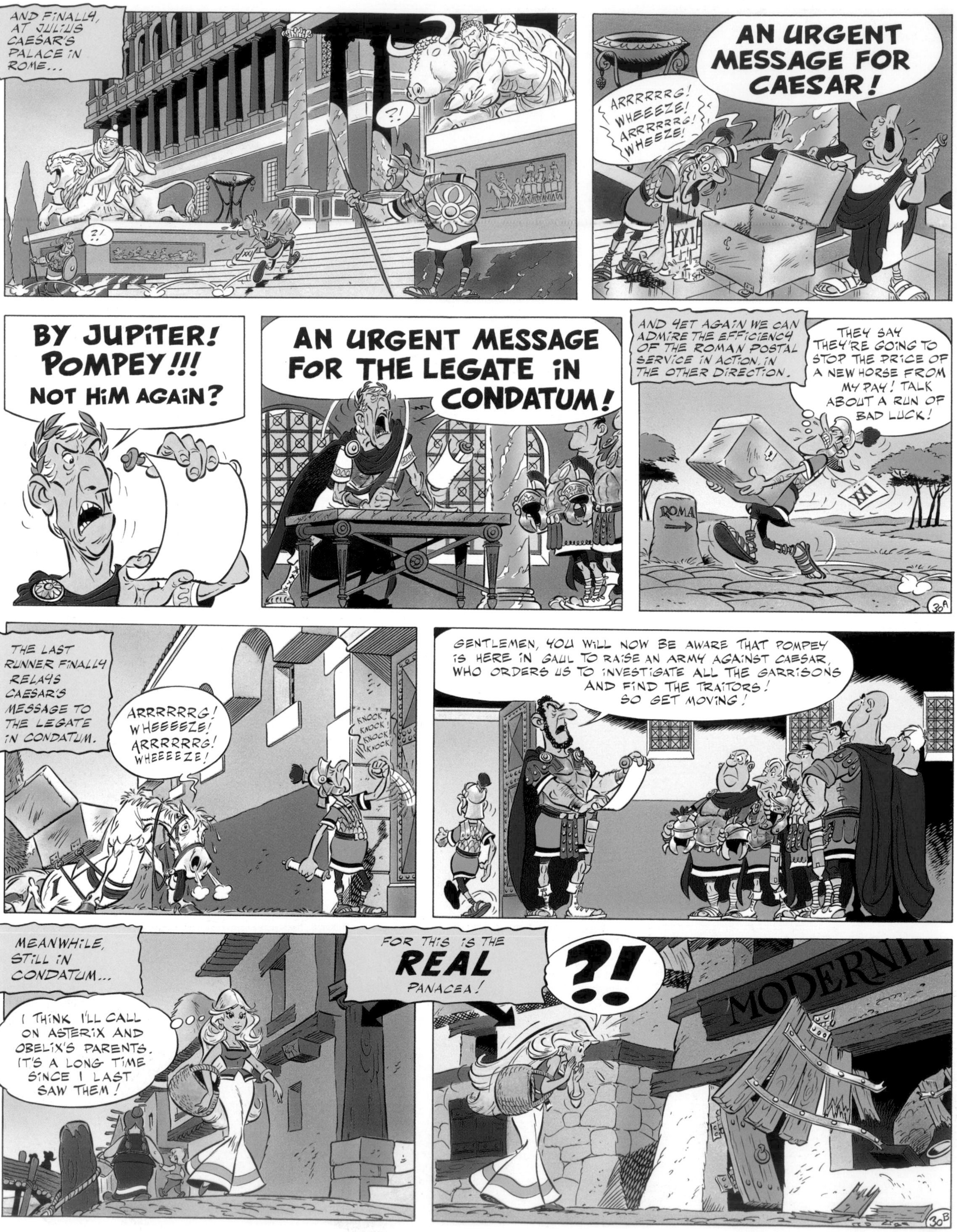
AND FINALLY, AT JULIUS CAESAR'S PALACE IN ROME...
?!
?!
AN URGENT MESSAGE FOR CAESAR!
ARRRRRRG! WHEEEZE! ARRRRRRG! WHEEZE!
XXI
BY JUPITER! POMPEY!!! NOT HIM AGAIN?
AN URGENT MESSAGE FOR THE LEGATE IN CONDATUM!
AND YET AGAIN WE CAN ADMIRE THE EFFICIENCY OF THE ROMAN POSTAL SERVICE IN ACTION, IN THE OTHER DIRECTION.
THEY SAY THEY'RE GOING TO STOP THE PRICE OF A NEW HORSE FROM MY PAY! TALK ABOUT A RUN OF BAD LUCK!
ROMA
XXI
THE LAST RUNNER FINALLY RELAYS CAESAR'S MESSAGE TO THE LEGATE IN CONDATUM.
ARRRRRRG! WHEEEEZE! ARRRRRRG! WHEEEEZE!
KNOCK KNOCK KNOCK KNOCK
GENTLEMEN, YOU WILL NOW BE AWARE THAT POMPEY IS HERE IN GAUL TO RAISE AN ARMY AGAINST CAESAR, WHO ORDERS US TO INVESTIGATE ALL THE GARRISONS AND FIND THE TRAITORS! SO GET MOVING!
MEANWHILE, STILL IN CONDATUM...
I THINK I'LL CALL ON ASTERIX AND OBELIX'S PARENTS. IT'S A LONG TIME SINCE I LAST SAW THEM!
FOR THIS IS THE REAL PANACEA!
?!
MODERNIT

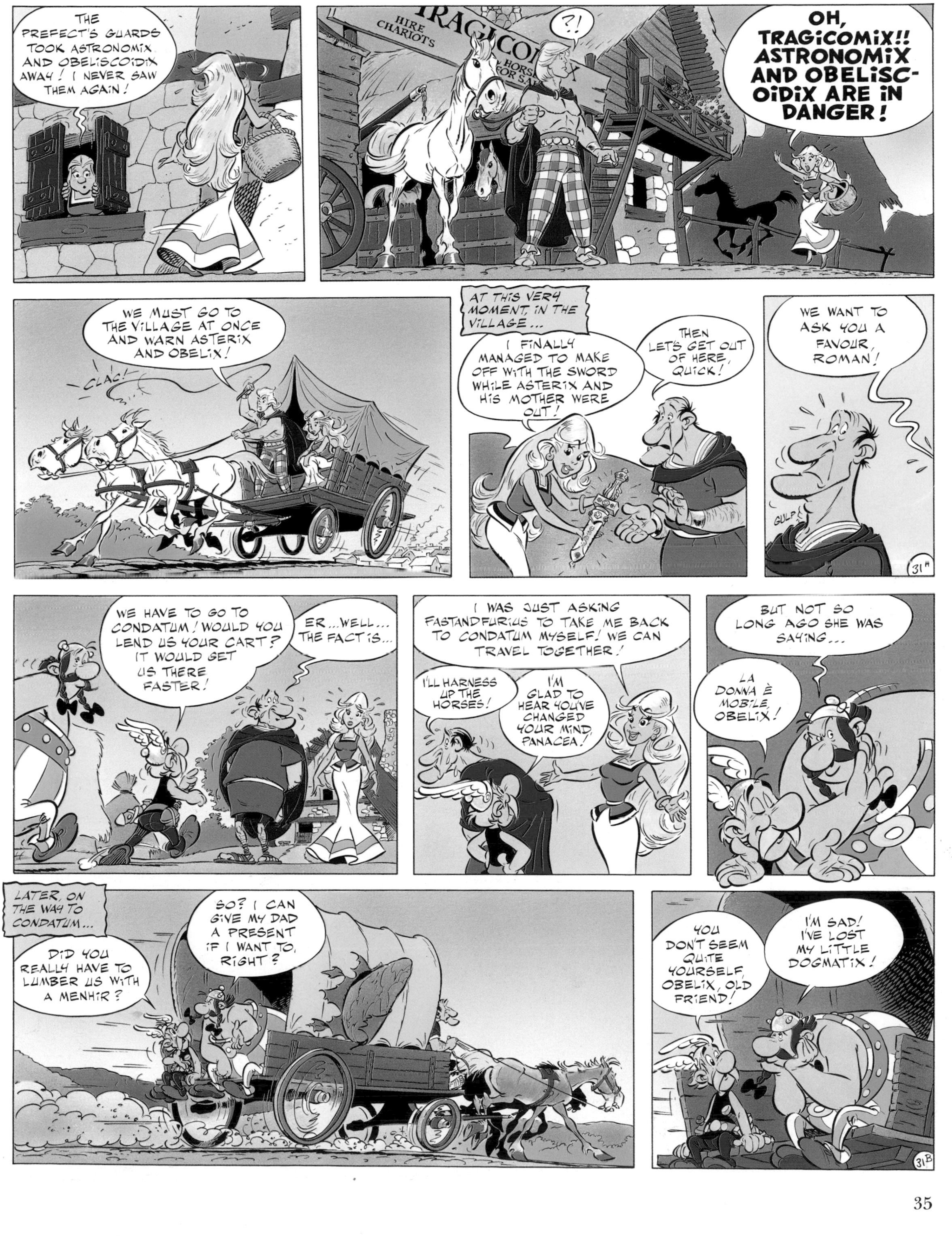
THE PREFECT'S GUARDS TOOK ASTRONOMIX AND OBELISCOIDIX AWAY! I NEVER SAW THEM AGAIN!
TRAGICOMIX
HIRE CHARIOTS
HORSES FOR SALE
?!
OH, TRAGICOMIX!! ASTRONOMIX AND OBELISCOIDIX ARE IN DANGER!
WE MUST GO TO THE VILLAGE AT ONCE AND WARN ASTERIX AND OBELIX!
CLAC!
AT THIS VERY MOMENT, IN THE VILLAGE...
I FINALLY MANAGED TO MAKE OFF WITH THE SWORD WHILE ASTERIX AND HIS MOTHER WERE OUT!
THEN LET'S GET OUT OF HERE, QUICK!
WE WANT TO ASK YOU A FAVOUR, ROMAN!
GULP!
WE HAVE TO GO TO CONDATUM! WOULD YOU LEND US YOUR CART? IT WOULD GET US THERE FASTER!
ER... WELL... THE FACT IS...
I WAS JUST ASKING FASTANDFURIUS TO TAKE ME BACK TO CONDATUM MYSELF! WE CAN TRAVEL TOGETHER!
I'LL HARNESS UP THE HORSES!
I'M GLAD TO HEAR YOU'VE CHANGED YOUR MIND, PANACEA!
BUT NOT SO LONG AGO SHE WAS SAYING...
LA DONNA È MOBILE, OBELIX!
LATER, ON THE WAY TO CONDATUM...
DID YOU REALLY HAVE TO LUMBER US WITH A MENHIR?
SO? I CAN GIVE MY DAD A PRESENT IF I WANT TO, RIGHT?
YOU DON'T SEEM QUITE YOURSELF OBELIX, OLD FRIEND!
I'M SAD! I'VE LOST MY LITTLE DOGMATIX!

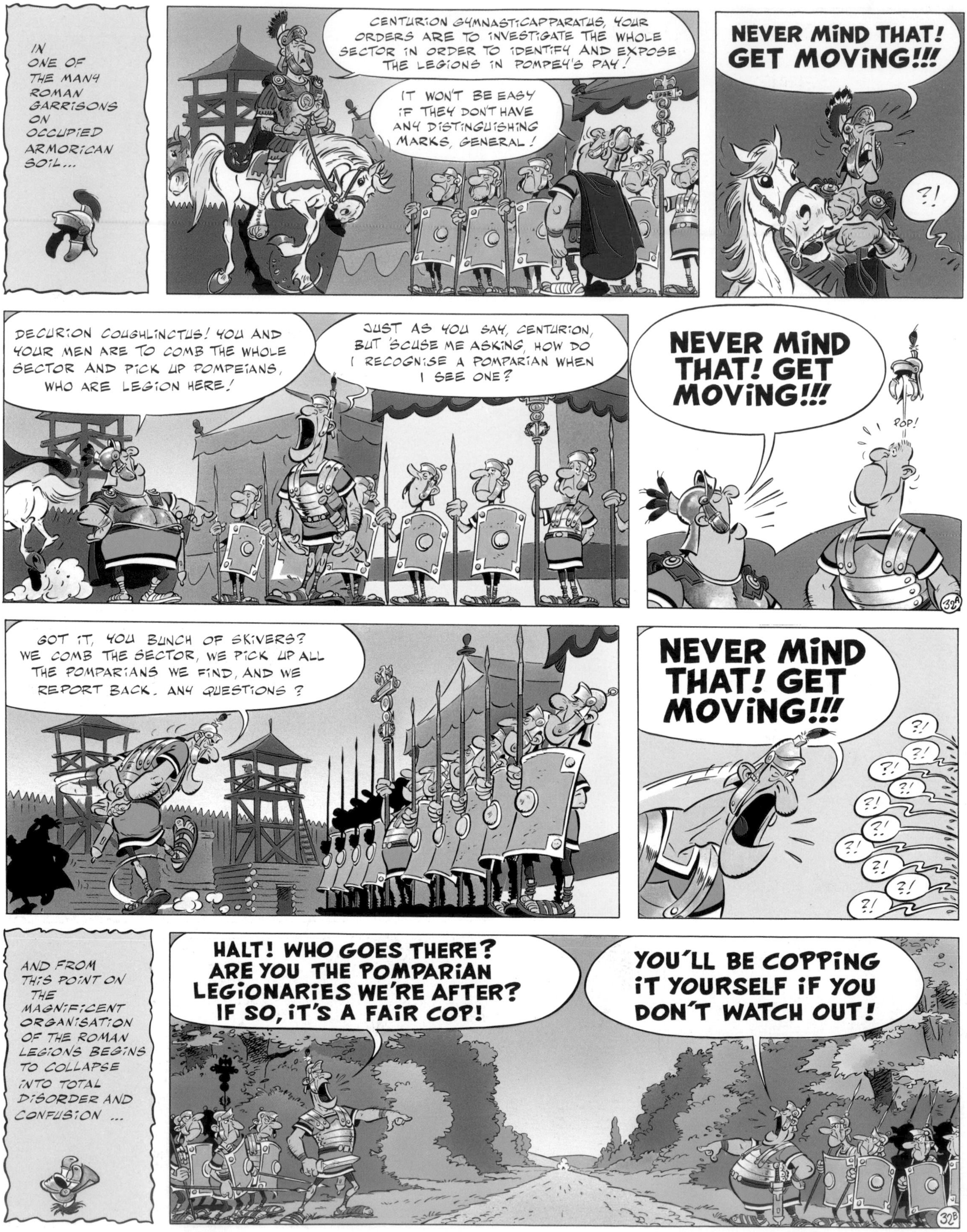

IN ONE OF THE MANY ROMAN GARRISONS ON OCCUPIED ARMORICAN SOIL...
CENTURION GYMNASTICAPPARATUS, YOUR ORDERS ARE TO INVESTIGATE THE WHOLE SECTOR IN ORDER TO IDENTIFY AND EXPOSE THE LEGIONS IN POMPEY'S PAY!
IT WON'T BE EASY IF THEY DON'T HAVE ANY DISTINGUISHING MARKS, GENERAL!
NEVER MIND THAT! GET MOVING!!!
?!
DECURION COUGHLINCTUS! YOU AND YOUR MEN ARE TO COMB THE WHOLE SECTOR AND PICK UP POMPEIANS, WHO ARE LEGION HERE!
JUST AS YOU SAY, CENTURION, BUT 'SCUSE ME ASKING, HOW DO I RECOGNISE A POMPARIAN WHEN I SEE ONE?
NEVER MIND THAT! GET MOVING!!!
POP!
GOT IT, YOU BUNCH OF SKIVERS? WE COMB THE SECTOR, WE PICK UP ALL THE POMPARIANS WE FIND, AND WE REPORT BACK. ANY QUESTIONS?
NEVER MIND THAT! GET MOVING!!!
?!
?!
?!
?!
?!
?!
?!
?!
?!
?!
AND FROM THIS POINT ON THE MAGNIFICENT ORGANISATION OF THE ROMAN LEGIONS BEGINS TO COLLAPSE INTO TOTAL DISORDER AND CONFUSION ...
HALT! WHO GOES THERE? ARE YOU THE POMPARIAN LEGIONARIES WE'RE AFTER? IF SO, IT'S A FAIR COP!
YOU'LL BE COPPING IT YOURSELF IF YOU DON'T WATCH OUT!

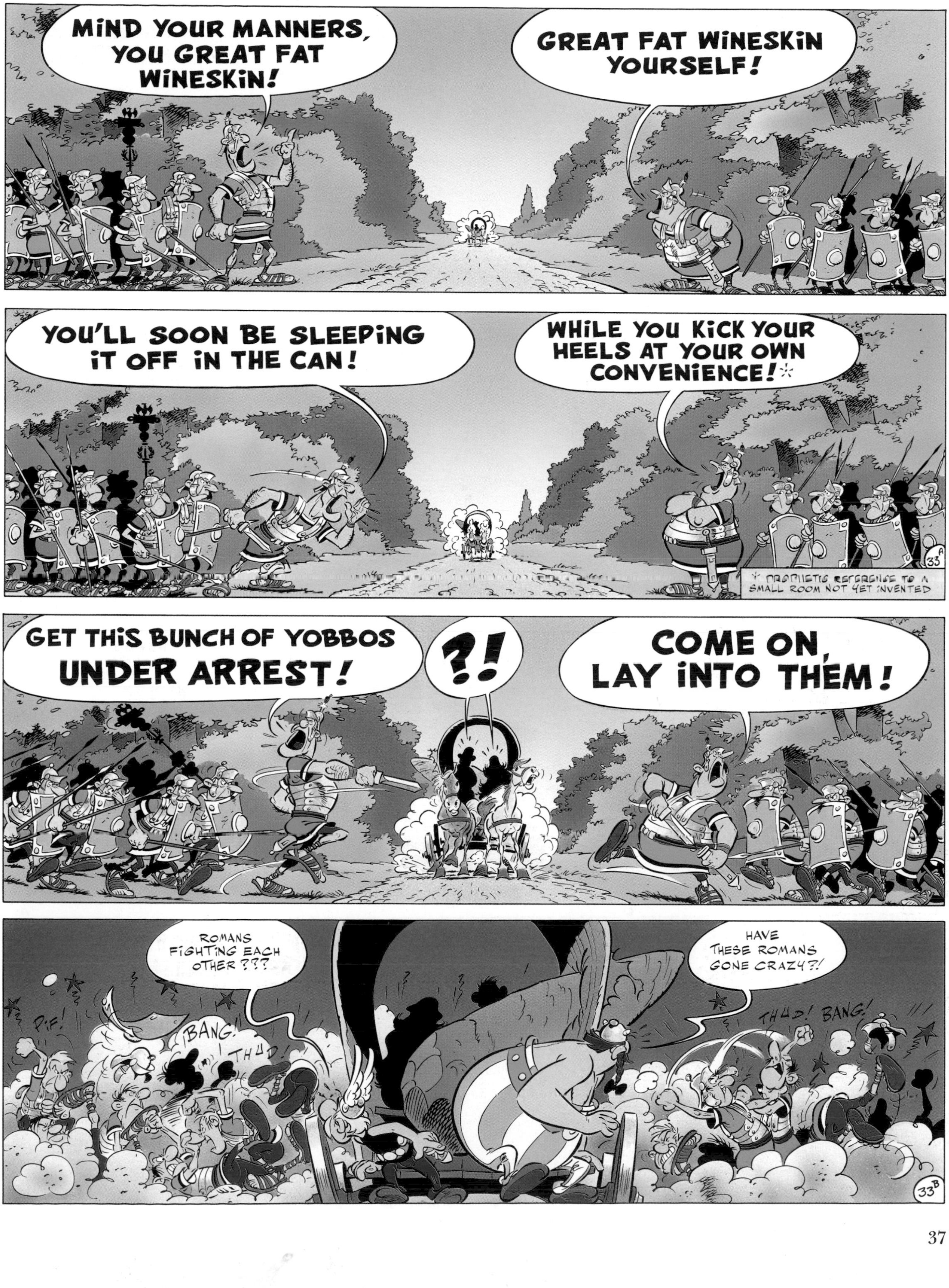
MIND YOUR MANNERS, YOU GREAT FAT WINESKIN!
GREAT FAT WINESKIN YOURSELF!
YOU'LL SOON BE SLEEPING IT OFF IN THE CAN!
WHILE YOU KICK YOUR HEELS AT YOUR OWN CONVENIENCE!*
* PROPHETIC REFERENCE TO A SMALL ROOM NOT YET INVENTED
GET THIS BUNCH OF YOBBOS UNDER ARREST!
?!
COME ON, LAY INTO THEM!
ROMANS FIGHTING EACH OTHER???
HAVE THESE ROMANS GONE CRAZY?!
PIF!
BANG!
THUD!
THUD! BANG!

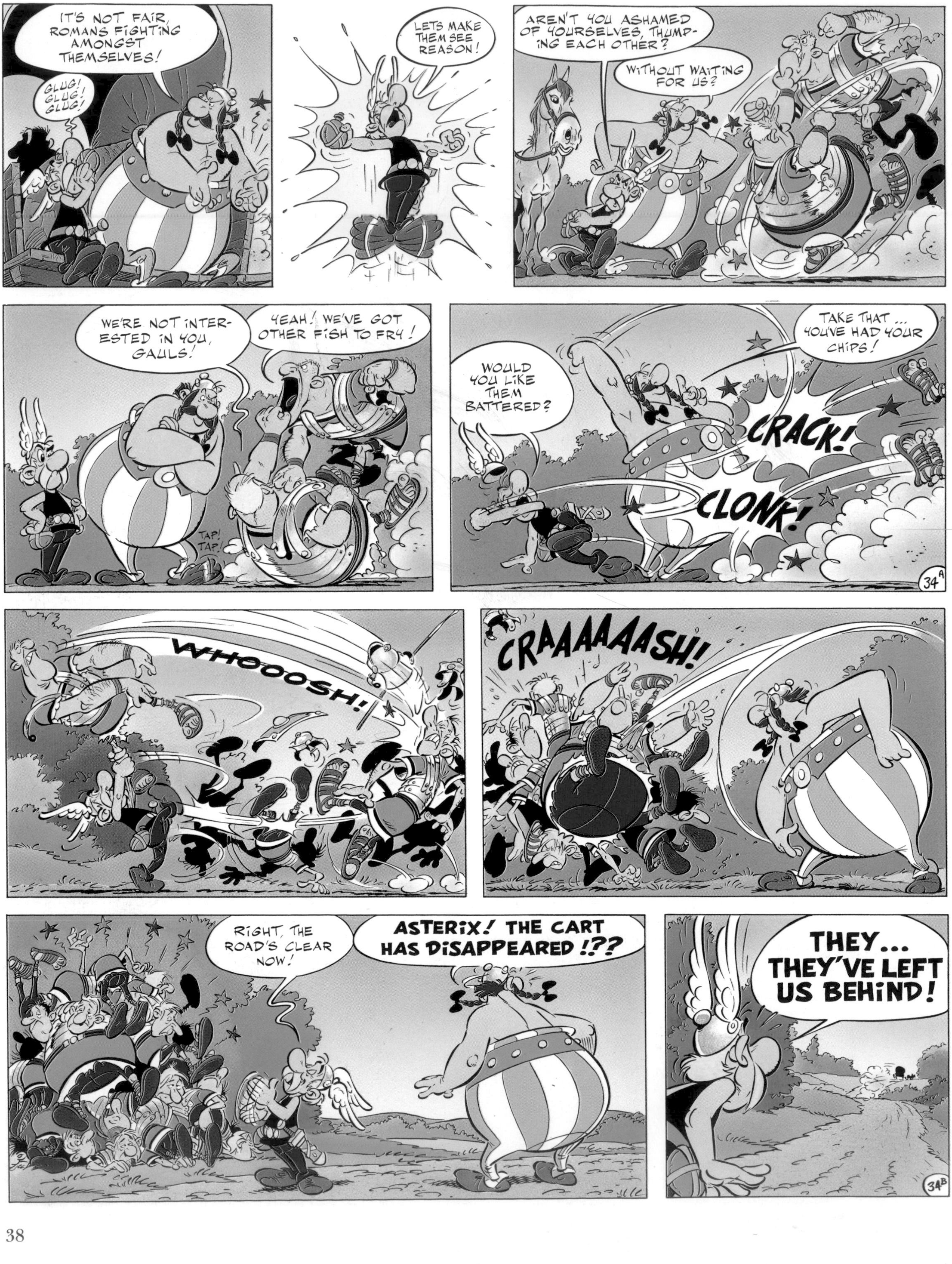
IT'S NOT FAIR, ROMANS FIGHTING AMONGST THEMSELVES!
GLUG! GLUG! GLUG!
LETS MAKE THEM SEE REASON!
AREN'T YOU ASHAMED OF YOURSELVES, THUMPING EACH OTHER?
WITHOUT WAITING FOR US?
WE'RE NOT INTERESTED IN YOU, GAULS!
YEAH! WE'VE GOT OTHER FISH TO FRY!
TAP! TAP!
WOULD YOU LIKE THEM BATTERED?
TAKE THAT ... YOU'VE HAD YOUR CHIPS!
CRACK!
CLONK!
34A
WHOOOOSH!
CRAAAAAASH!
RIGHT, THE ROAD'S CLEAR NOW!
ASTERIX! THE CART HAS DISAPPEARED!??
THEY... THEY'VE LEFT US BEHIND!
34B

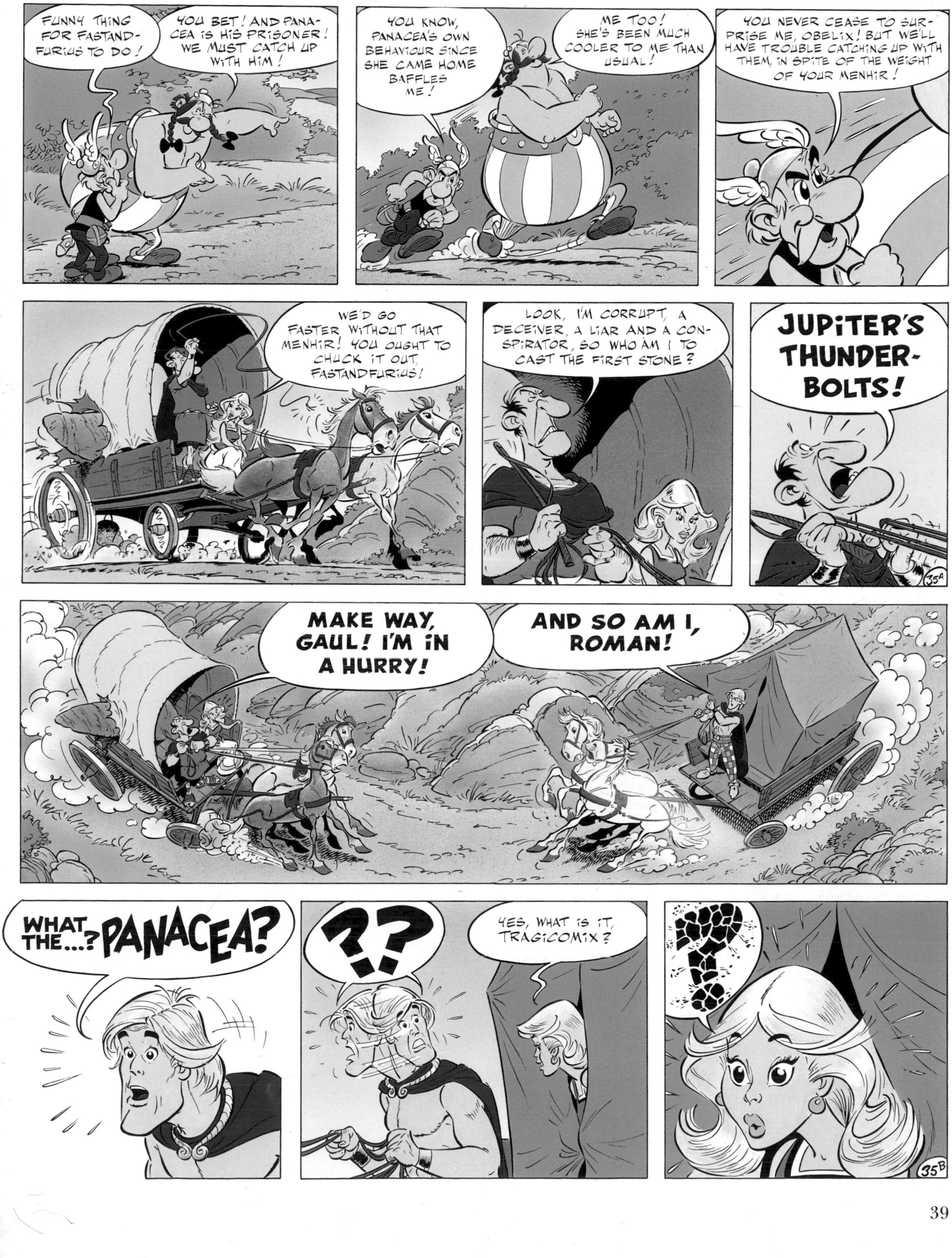

FUNNY THING FOR FASTANDFURIUS TO DO!
YOU BET! AND PANACEA IS HIS PRISONER! WE MUST CATCH UP WITH HIM!
YOU KNOW, PANACEA'S OWN BEHAVIOUR SINCE SHE CAME HOME BAFFLES ME!
ME TOO! SHE'S BEEN MUCH COOLER TO ME THAN USUAL!
YOU NEVER CEASE TO SURPRISE ME, OBELIX! BUT WE'LL HAVE TROUBLE CATCHING UP WITH THEM, IN SPITE OF THE WEIGHT OF YOUR MENHIR!
WE'D GO FASTER WITHOUT THAT MENHIR! YOU OUGHT TO CHUCK IT OUT, FASTANDFURIUS!
LOOK, I'M CORRUPT, A DECEIVER, A LIAR AND A CONSPIRATOR, SO WHO AM I TO CAST THE FIRST STONE?
JUPITER'S THUNDERBOLTS!
35A
MAKE WAY, GAUL! I'M IN A HURRY!
AND SO AM I, ROMAN!
WHAT THE...? PANACEA?
??
YES, WHAT IS IT, TRAGICOMIX?
35B

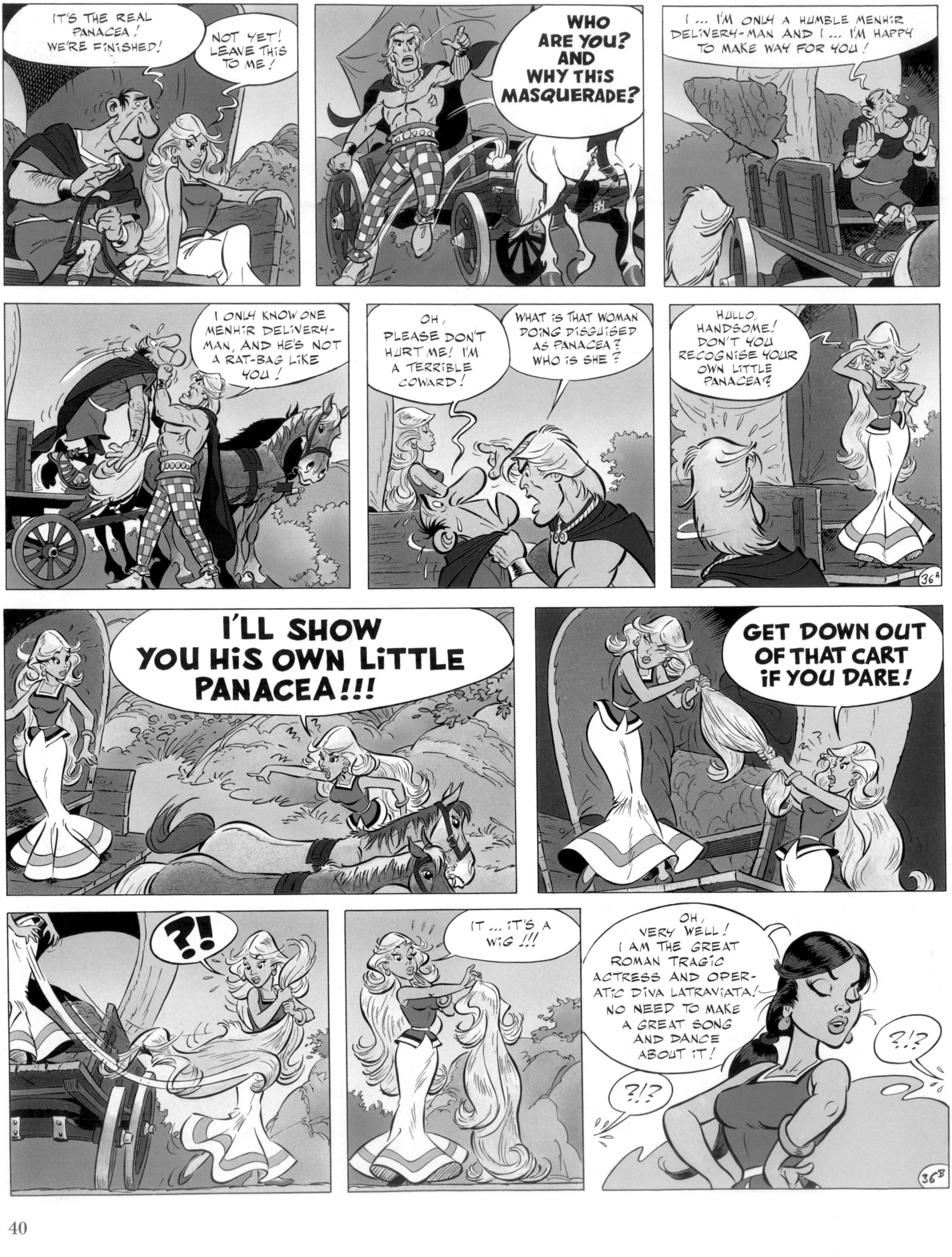
IT'S THE REAL PANACEA! WE'RE FINISHED!
NOT YET! LEAVE THIS TO ME!
WHO ARE YOU? AND WHY THIS MASQUERADE?
I ... I'M ONLY A HUMBLE MENHIR DELIVERY-MAN AND I ... I'M HAPPY TO MAKE WAY FOR YOU!
I ONLY KNOW ONE MENHIR DELIVERY-MAN, AND HE'S NOT A RAT-BAG LIKE YOU!
OH, PLEASE DON'T HURT ME! I'M A TERRIBLE COWARD!
WHAT IS THAT WOMAN DOING DISGUISED AS PANACEA? WHO IS SHE?
HULLO, HANDSOME! DON'T YOU RECOGNISE YOUR OWN LITTLE PANACEA?
36A
I'LL SHOW YOU HIS OWN LITTLE PANACEA!!!
GET DOWN OUT OF THAT CART IF YOU DARE!
?!
IT ... IT'S A WIG!!!
OH, VERY WELL! I AM THE GREAT ROMAN TRAGIC ACTRESS AND OPERATIC DIVA LATRAVIATA! NO NEED TO MAKE A GREAT SONG AND DANCE ABOUT IT!
?!?
?!?
36B

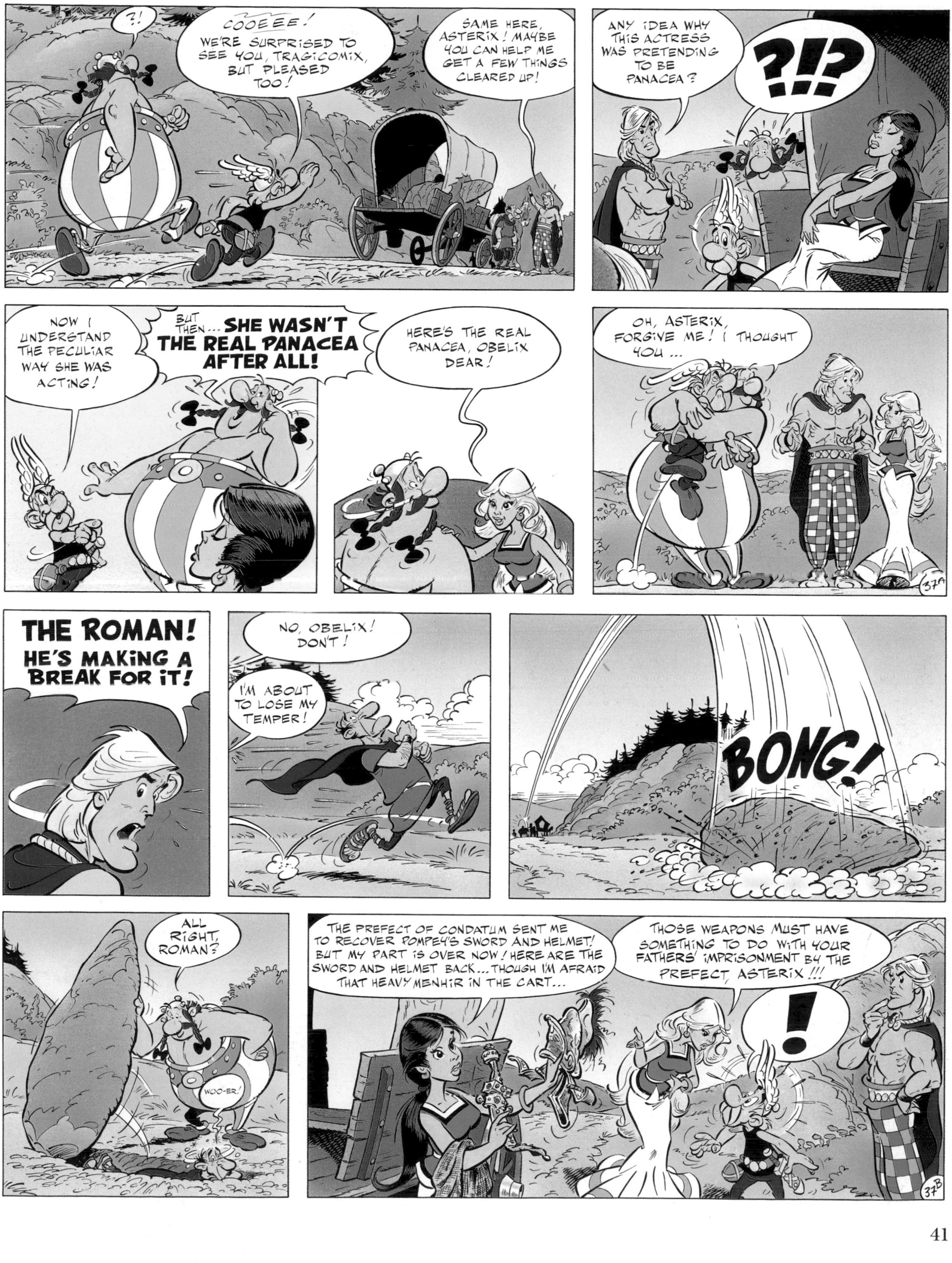
?!
COOEEE! WE'RE SURPRISED TO SEE YOU, TRAGICOMIX, BUT PLEASED TOO!
SAME HERE, ASTERIX! MAYBE YOU CAN HELP ME GET A FEW THINGS CLEARED UP!
ANY IDEA WHY THIS ACTRESS WAS PRETENDING TO BE PANACEA?
?!!?
NOW I UNDERSTAND THE PECULIAR WAY SHE WAS ACTING!
BUT THEN... SHE WASN'T THE REAL PANACEA AFTER ALL!
HERE'S THE REAL PANACEA, OBELIX DEAR!
OH, ASTERIX, FORGIVE ME! I THOUGHT YOU...
THE ROMAN! HE'S MAKING A BREAK FOR IT!
NO, OBELIX! DON'T!
I'M ABOUT TO LOSE MY TEMPER!
BONG!
ALL RIGHT, ROMAN?
WOO-ER!
THE PREFECT OF CONDATUM SENT ME TO RECOVER POMPEY'S SWORD AND HELMET! BUT MY PART IS OVER NOW! HERE ARE THE SWORD AND HELMET BACK... THOUGH I'M AFRAID THAT HEAVY MENHIR IN THE CART...
THOSE WEAPONS MUST HAVE SOMETHING TO DO WITH YOUR FATHERS' IMPRISONMENT BY THE PREFECT, ASTERIX!!!
!

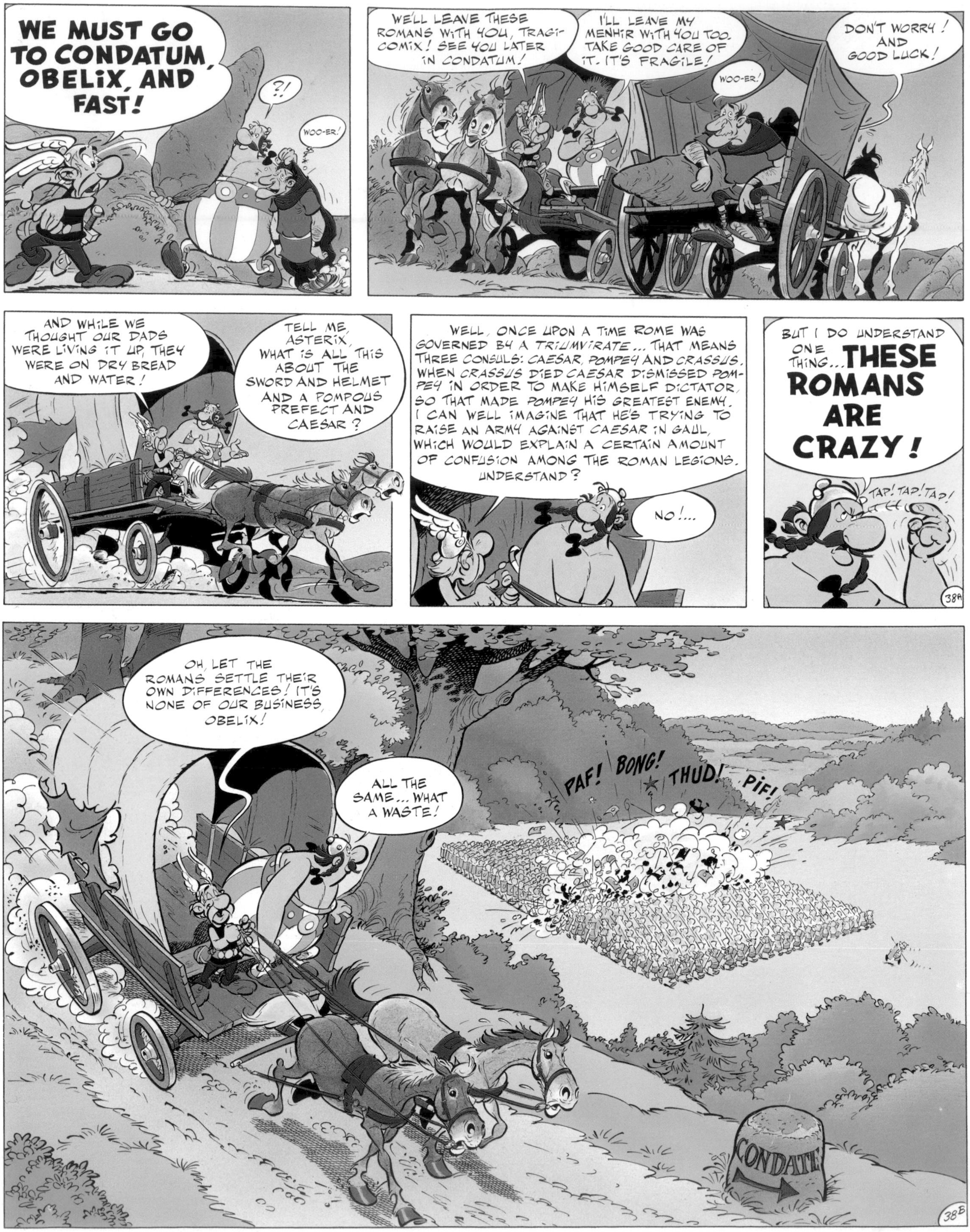
WE MUST GO TO CONDATUM, OBELIX, AND FAST!
?!
WOO-ER!
WE'LL LEAVE THESE ROMANS WITH YOU, TRAGICOMIX! SEE YOU LATER IN CONDATUM!
I'LL LEAVE MY MENHIR WITH YOU TOO. TAKE GOOD CARE OF IT. IT'S FRAGILE!
WOO-ER!
DON'T WORRY! AND GOOD LUCK!
AND WHILE WE THOUGHT OUR DADS WERE LIVING IT UP, THEY WERE ON DRY BREAD AND WATER!
TELL ME, ASTERIX, WHAT IS ALL THIS ABOUT THE SWORD AND HELMET AND A POMPOUS PREFECT AND CAESAR?
WELL, ONCE UPON A TIME ROME WAS GOVERNED BY A TRIUMVIRATE... THAT MEANS THREE CONSULS: CAESAR, POMPEY AND CRASSUS. WHEN CRASSUS DIED CAESAR DISMISSED POMPEY IN ORDER TO MAKE HIMSELF DICTATOR, SO THAT MADE POMPEY HIS GREATEST ENEMY. I CAN WELL IMAGINE THAT HE'S TRYING TO RAISE AN ARMY AGAINST CAESAR IN GAUL, WHICH WOULD EXPLAIN A CERTAIN AMOUNT OF CONFUSION AMONG THE ROMAN LEGIONS. UNDERSTAND?
NO!...
BUT I DO UNDERSTAND ONE THING... THESE ROMANS ARE CRAZY!
TAP! TAP! TAP!
38A
OH, LET THE ROMANS SETTLE THEIR OWN DIFFERENCES! IT'S NONE OF OUR BUSINESS, OBELIX!
ALL THE SAME... WHAT A WASTE!
PAF! BONG! THUD! PIF!
CONDATE
38B

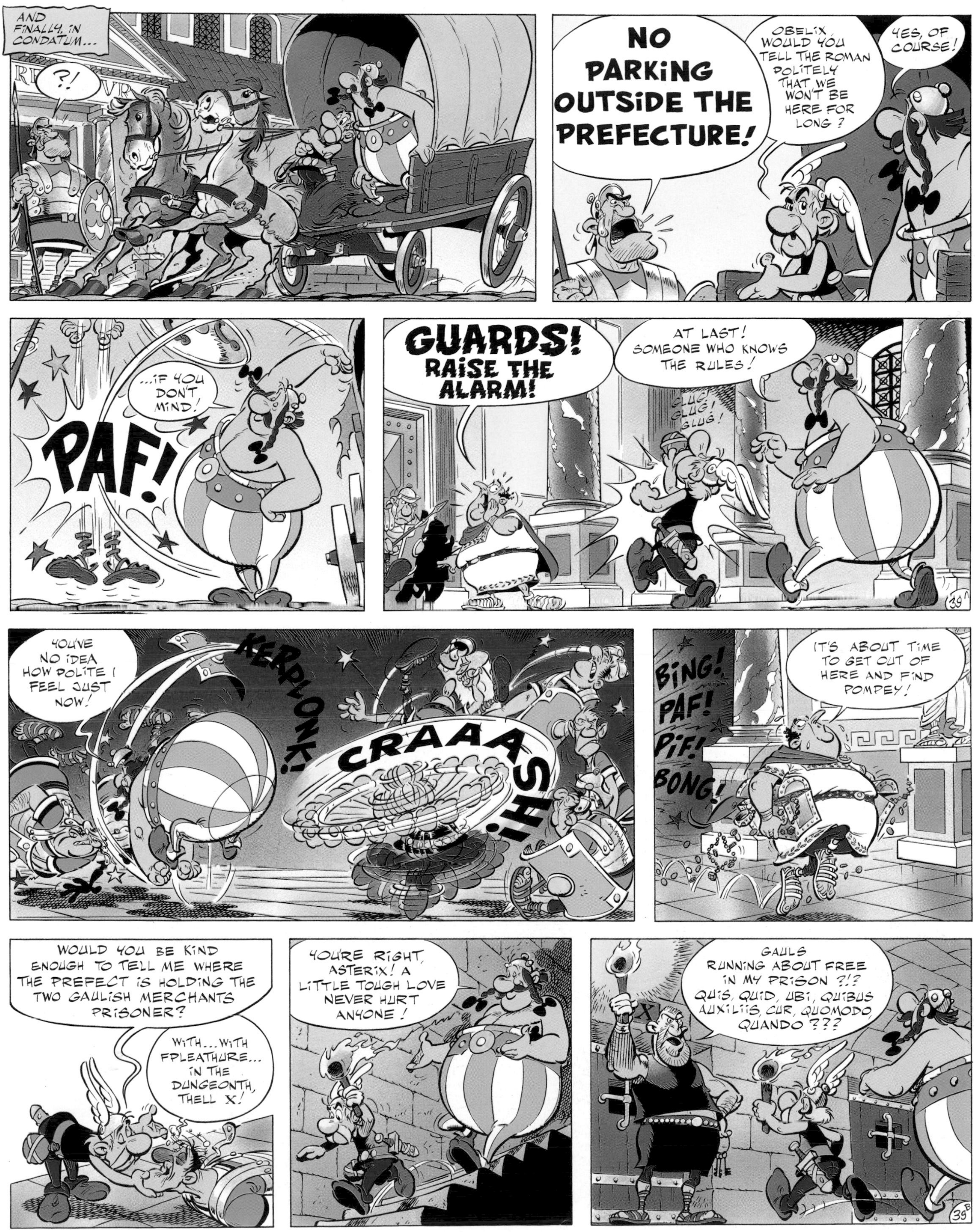
AND FINALLY, IN CONDATUM...
?!
NO PARKING OUTSIDE THE PREFECTURE!
OBELIX, WOULD YOU TELL THE ROMAN POLITELY THAT WE WON'T BE HERE FOR LONG?
YES, OF COURSE!
...IF YOU DON'T MIND!
PAF!
GUARDS! RAISE THE ALARM!
AT LAST! SOMEONE WHO KNOWS THE RULES!
GLUG! GLUG! GLUG!
YOU'VE NO IDEA HOW POLITE I FEEL JUST NOW!
KERPLONK!
CRAAASH!
BING! PAF! PIF! BONG!
IT'S ABOUT TIME TO GET OUT OF HERE AND FIND POMPEY!
WOULD YOU BE KIND ENOUGH TO TELL ME WHERE THE PREFECT IS HOLDING THE TWO GAULISH MERCHANTS PRISONER?
WITH... WITH FPLEATHURE... IN THE DUNGEONTH, THELL X!
YOU'RE RIGHT, ASTERIX! A LITTLE TOUGH LOVE NEVER HURT ANYONE!
GAULS RUNNING ABOUT FREE IN MY PRISON ?!? QUIS, QUID, UBI, QUIBUS AUXILIIS, CUR, QUOMODO, QUANDO ???

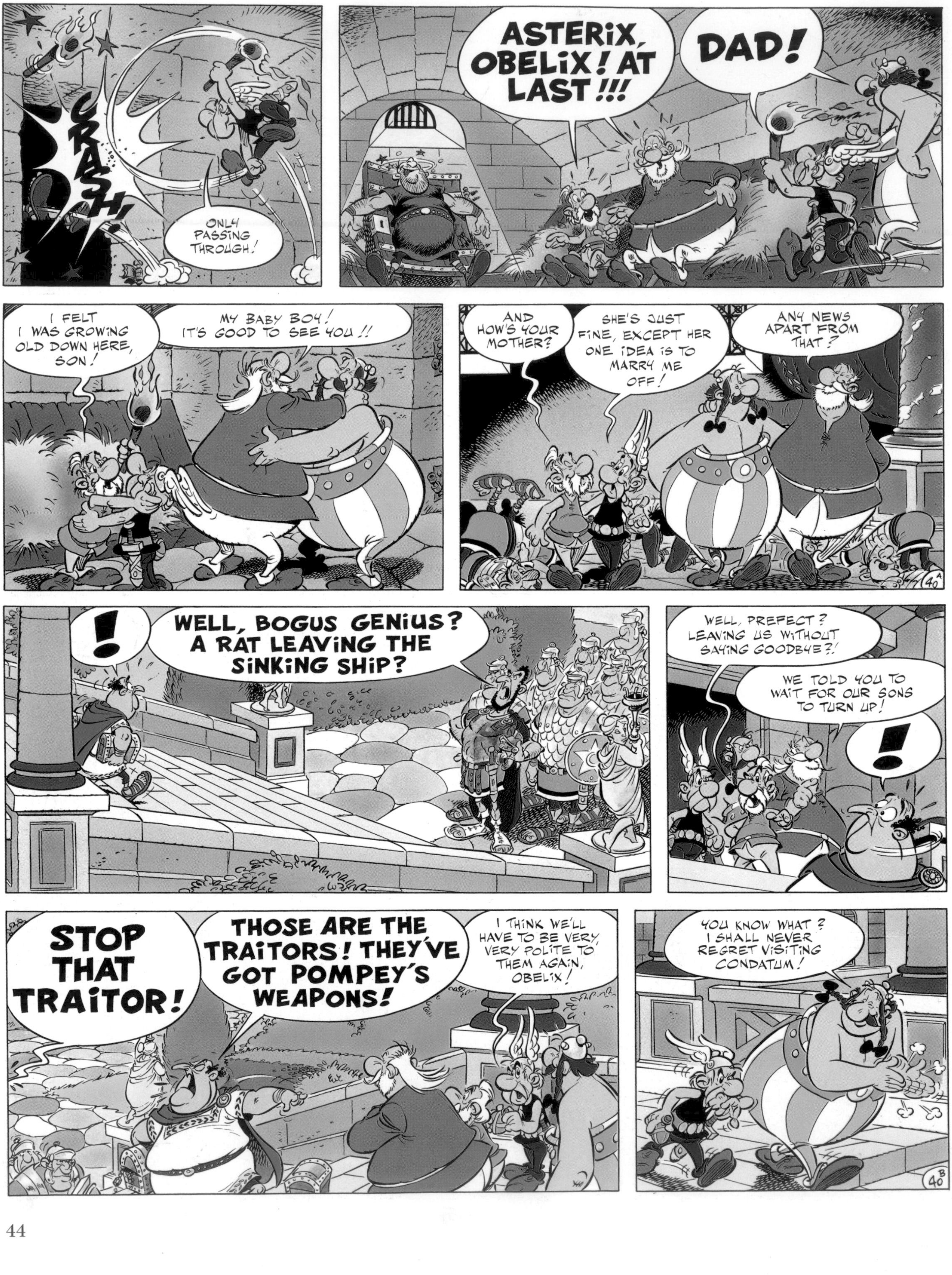
CRASH!
ONLY PASSING THROUGH!
ASTERIX, OBELIX! AT LAST!!!
DAD!
I FELT I WAS GROWING OLD DOWN HERE, SON!
MY BABY BOY! IT'S GOOD TO SEE YOU!!
AND HOW'S YOUR MOTHER?
SHE'S JUST FINE, EXCEPT HER ONE IDEA IS TO MARRY ME OFF!
ANY NEWS APART FROM THAT?
!
WELL, BOGUS GENIUS? A RAT LEAVING THE SINKING SHIP?
WELL, PREFECT? LEAVING US WITHOUT SAYING GOODBYE?!
WE TOLD YOU TO WAIT FOR OUR SONS TO TURN UP!
!
STOP THAT TRAITOR!
THOSE ARE THE TRAITORS! THEY'VE GOT POMPEY'S WEAPONS!
I THINK WE'LL HAVE TO BE VERY, VERY POLITE TO THEM AGAIN, OBELIX!
YOU KNOW WHAT? I SHALL NEVER REGRET VISITING CONDATUM!

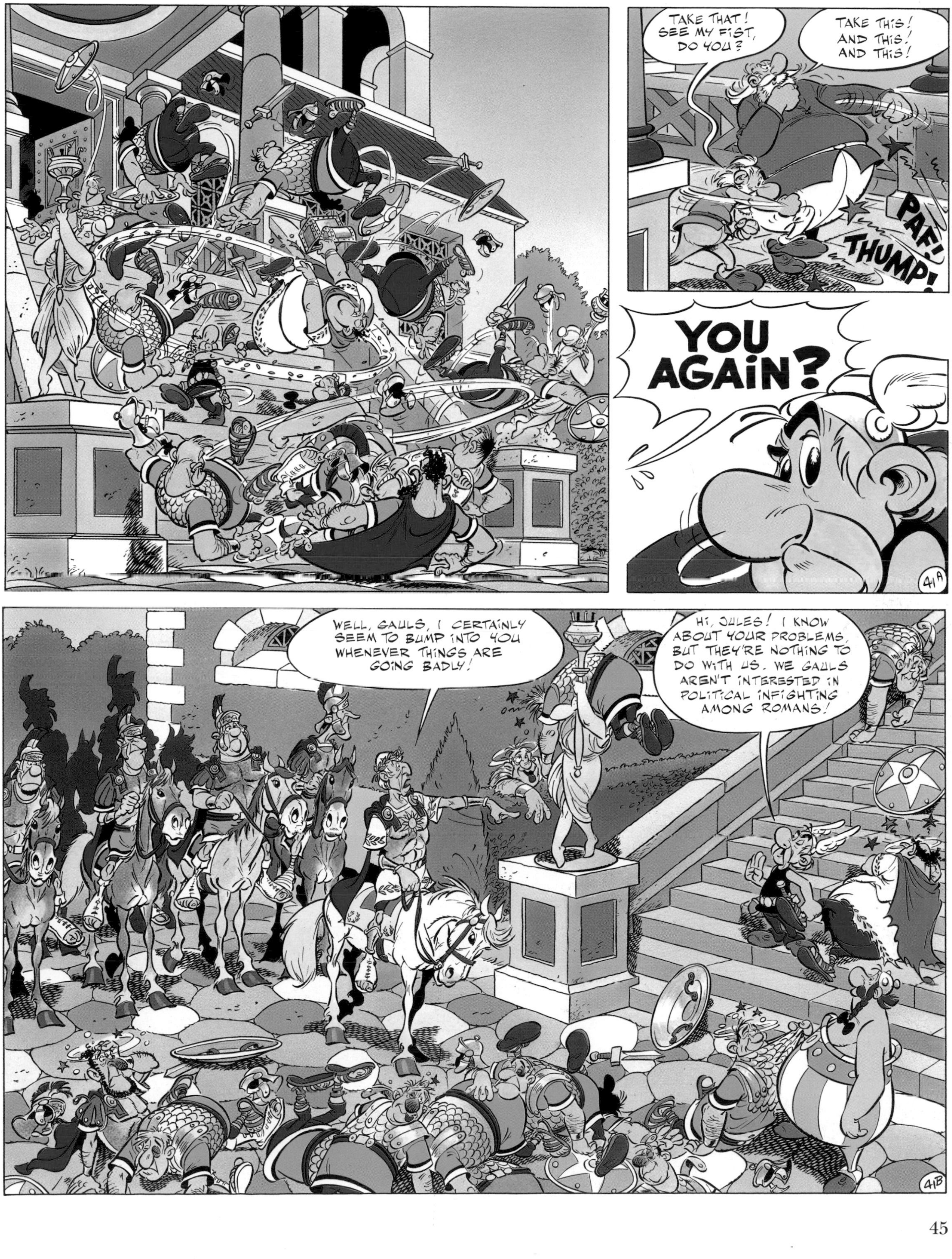
TAKE THAT! SEE MY FIST, DO YOU?
TAKE THIS! AND THIS! AND THIS!
PAF!
THUMP!
YOU AGAIN?
41A
WELL, GAULS, I CERTAINLY SEEM TO BUMP INTO YOU WHENEVER THINGS ARE GOING BADLY!
HI, JULES! I KNOW ABOUT YOUR PROBLEMS, BUT THEY'RE NOTHING TO DO WITH US. WE GAULS AREN'T INTERESTED IN POLITICAL INFIGHTING AMONG ROMANS!
41B

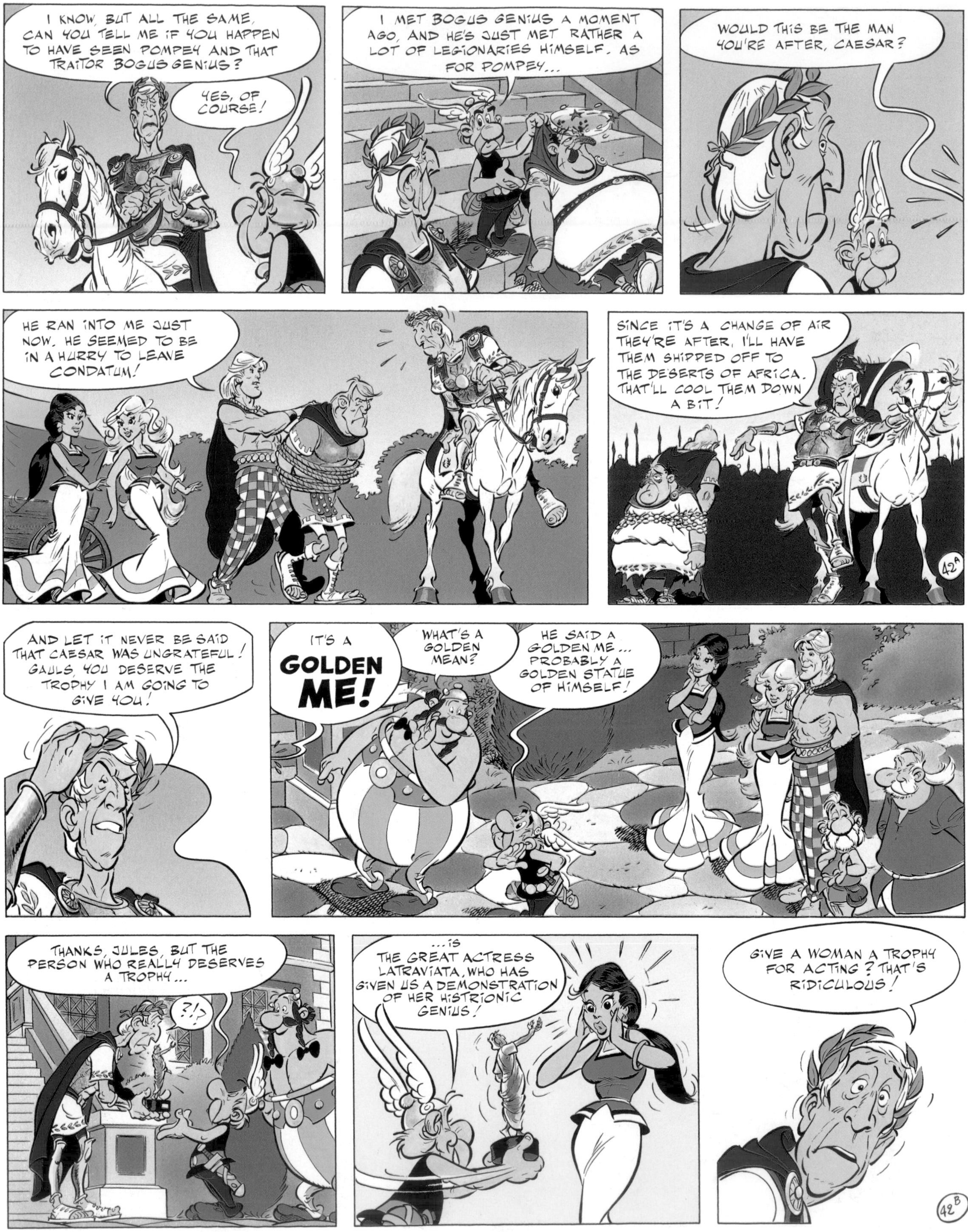
I KNOW, BUT ALL THE SAME, CAN YOU TELL ME IF YOU HAPPEN TO HAVE SEEN POMPEY AND THAT TRAITOR BOGUS GENIUS?
YES, OF COURSE!
I MET BOGUS GENIUS A MOMENT AGO, AND HE'S JUST MET RATHER A LOT OF LEGIONARIES HIMSELF. AS FOR POMPEY...
WOULD THIS BE THE MAN YOU'RE AFTER, CAESAR?
HE RAN INTO ME JUST NOW. HE SEEMED TO BE IN A HURRY TO LEAVE CONDATUM!
SINCE IT'S A CHANGE OF AIR THEY'RE AFTER, I'LL HAVE THEM SHIPPED OFF TO THE DESERTS OF AFRICA. THAT'LL COOL THEM DOWN A BIT!
42A
AND LET IT NEVER BE SAID THAT CAESAR WAS UNGRATEFUL! GAULS, YOU DESERVE THE TROPHY I AM GOING TO GIVE YOU!
IT'S A GOLDEN ME!
WHAT'S A GOLDEN MEAN?
HE SAID A GOLDEN ME... PROBABLY A GOLDEN STATUE OF HIMSELF!
THANKS, JULES, BUT THE PERSON WHO REALLY DESERVES A TROPHY...
?!?
...IS THE GREAT ACTRESS LATRAVIATA, WHO HAS GIVEN US A DEMONSTRATION OF HER HISTRIONIC GENIUS!
GIVE A WOMAN A TROPHY FOR ACTING? THAT'S RIDICULOUS!
42B

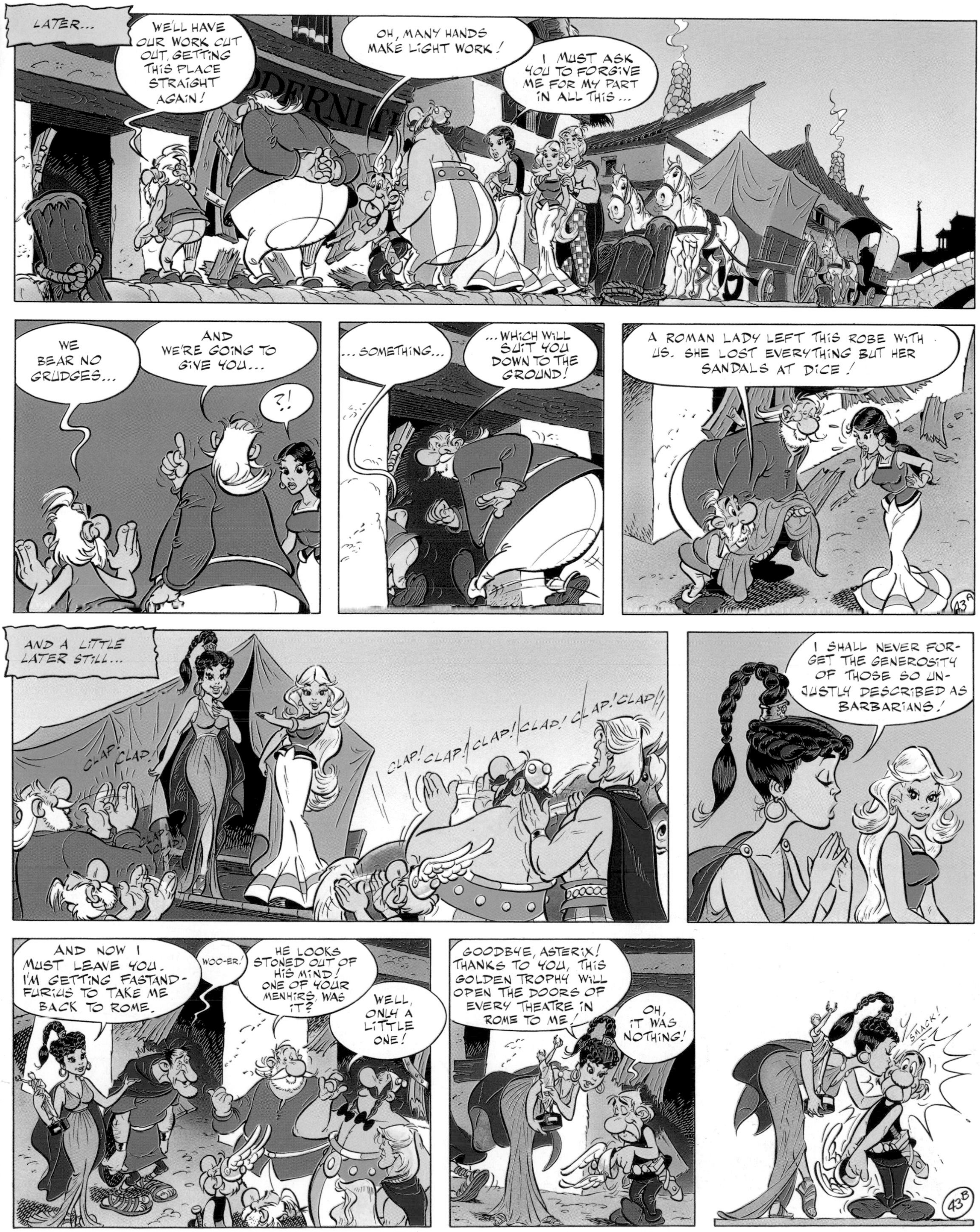

LATER...
WE'LL HAVE OUR WORK CUT OUT, GETTING THIS PLACE STRAIGHT AGAIN!
OH, MANY HANDS MAKE LIGHT WORK!
I MUST ASK YOU TO FORGIVE ME FOR MY PART IN ALL THIS...
WE BEAR NO GRUDGES...
AND WE'RE GOING TO GIVE YOU...
?!
...SOMETHING...
...WHICH WILL SUIT YOU DOWN TO THE GROUND!
A ROMAN LADY LEFT THIS ROBE WITH US. SHE LOST EVERYTHING BUT HER SANDALS AT DICE!
AND A LITTLE LATER STILL...
CLAP! CLAP!
CLAP! CLAP!
CLAP! CLAP! CLAP! CLAP! CLAP! CLAP!
I SHALL NEVER FORGET THE GENEROSITY OF THOSE SO UNJUSTLY DESCRIBED AS BARBARIANS!
AND NOW I MUST LEAVE YOU. I'M GETTING FASTANDFURIUS TO TAKE ME BACK TO ROME.
WOO-ER!
HE LOOKS STONED OUT OF HIS MIND! ONE OF YOUR MENHIRS, WAS IT?
WELL, ONLY A LITTLE ONE!
GOODBYE, ASTERIX! THANKS TO YOU, THIS GOLDEN TROPHY WILL OPEN THE DOORS OF EVERY THEATRE IN ROME TO ME!
OH, IT WAS NOTHING!
SMACK!

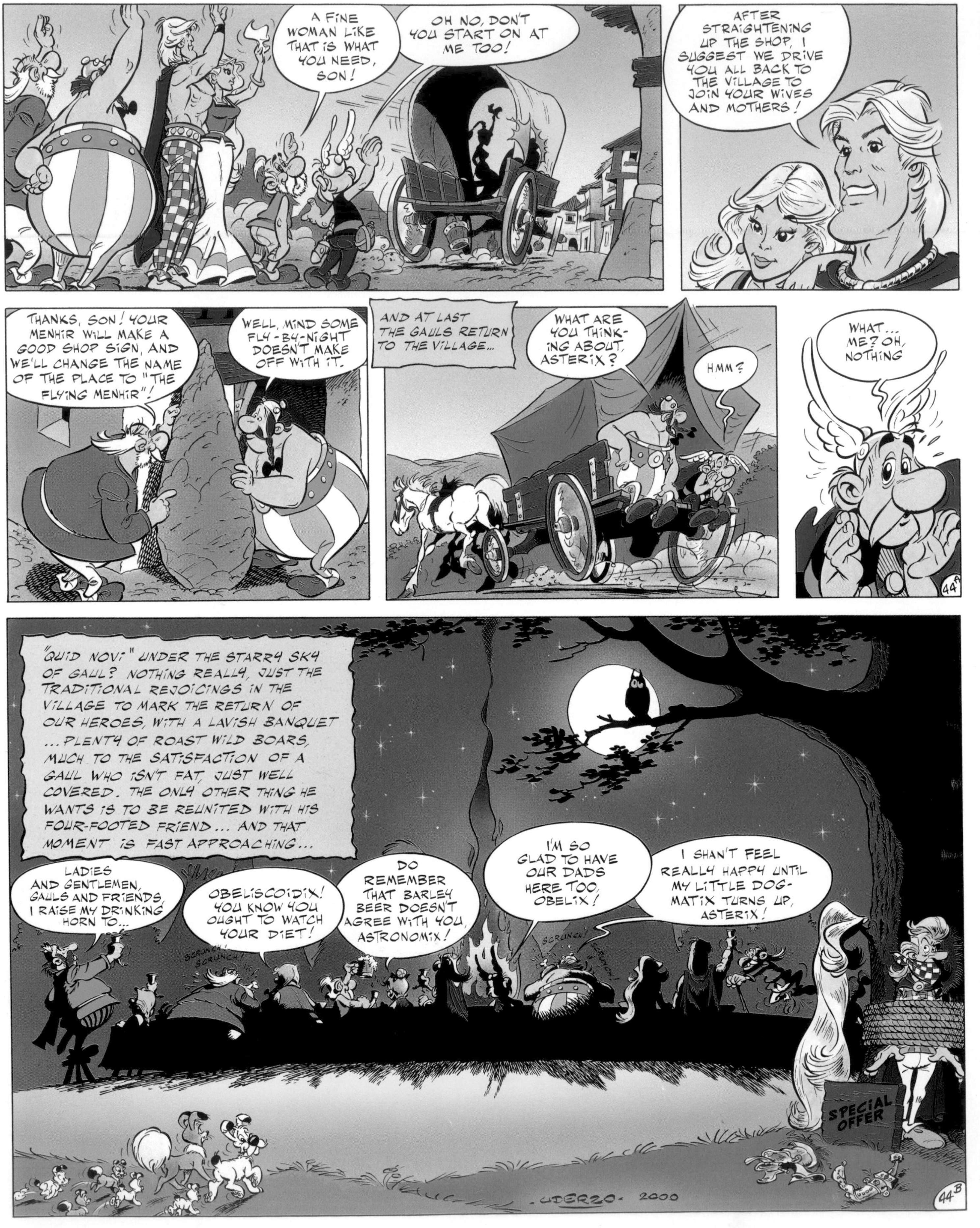
A FINE WOMAN LIKE THAT IS WHAT YOU NEED, SON!
OH NO, DON'T YOU START ON AT ME TOO!
AFTER STRAIGHTENING UP THE SHOP, I SUGGEST WE DRIVE YOU ALL BACK TO THE VILLAGE TO JOIN YOUR WIVES AND MOTHERS!
THANKS, SON! YOUR MENHIR WILL MAKE A GOOD SHOP SIGN, AND WE'LL CHANGE THE NAME OF THE PLACE TO "THE FLYING MENHIR"!
WELL, MIND SOME FLY-BY-NIGHT DOESN'T MAKE OFF WITH IT.
AND AT LAST THE GAULS RETURN TO THE VILLAGE...
WHAT ARE YOU THINKING ABOUT, ASTERIX?
HMM?
WHAT... ME? OH, NOTHING
44A
"QUID NOVI" UNDER THE STARRY SKY OF GAUL? NOTHING REALLY, JUST THE TRADITIONAL REJOICINGS IN THE VILLAGE TO MARK THE RETURN OF OUR HEROES, WITH A LAVISH BANQUET ... PLENTY OF ROAST WILD BOARS, MUCH TO THE SATISFACTION OF A GAUL WHO ISN'T FAT, JUST WELL COVERED. THE ONLY OTHER THING HE WANTS IS TO BE REUNITED WITH HIS FOUR-FOOTED FRIEND... AND THAT MOMENT IS FAST APPROACHING...
LADIES AND GENTLEMEN, GAULS AND FRIENDS, I RAISE MY DRINKING HORN TO...
OBELISCOIDIX! YOU KNOW YOU OUGHT TO WATCH YOUR DIET!
DO REMEMBER THAT BARLEY BEER DOESN'T AGREE WITH YOU, ASTRONOMIX!
I'M SO GLAD TO HAVE OUR DADS HERE TOO, OBELIX!
I SHAN'T FEEL REALLY HAPPY UNTIL MY LITTLE DOGMATIX TURNS UP, ASTERIX!
SCRUNCH! SCRUNCH!
SCRUNCH! SCRUNCH!
SPECIAL OFFER
UDERZO 2000
44B

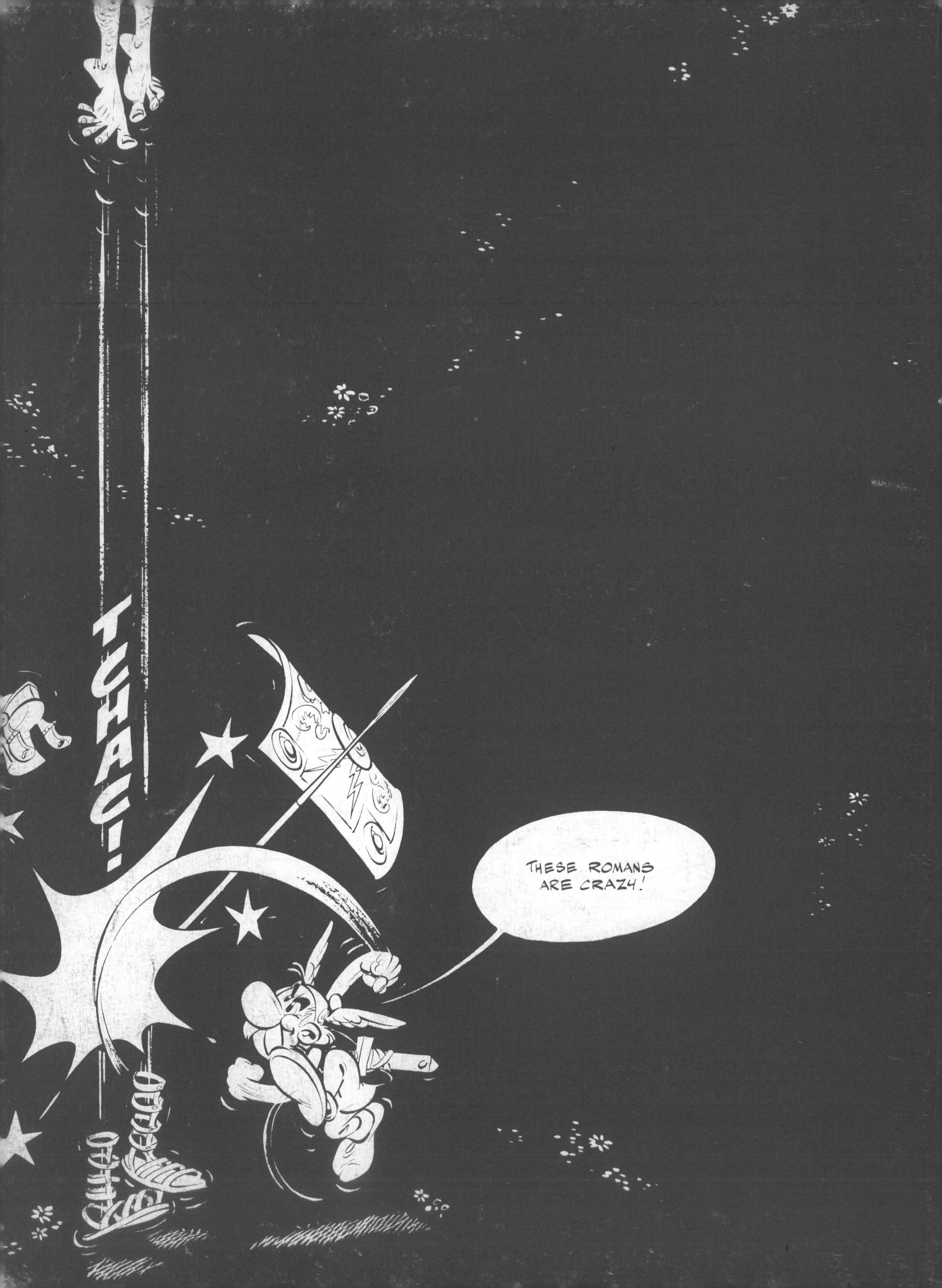
THACK!!
THESE ROMANS ARE CRAZY!